The Sheltering Rain

Hanmura Ryō

The Sheltering Rain (雨やどり)
Hanmura Ryō (半村 良)

Copyright @ 1975 Hanmura Ryō
Translation copyright © 2019 Jim Hubbert

This edition copyright © 2019 Kurodahan Press. All rights reserved. No part of this publication may be reproduced in whole or in part, or stored in a retrieval system, or transmitted in any form or by any means, electronic, mechanical, photocopying, recording, or otherwise, without written permission from the publisher.

FG-JP0060L
ISBN: 978-4-909473-50-9

Edited by Sabine Seiler
Cover by Johnny Wales
Rear photo: PRO Stock Professional/Shutterstock.com

KURODAHAN PRESS
kurodahan.com

The Sheltering Rain

Hanmura Ryō

Translated by
Jim Hubbert

Kurodahan Press
2019

Contents

Introduction	vii
Pushover	1
The Two of Us	31
The Sage of Shinjuku	53
A Man of Shinjuku	77
Night Train	99
The Sheltering Rain	107
Back to the Old Days	131
Fooltown	155
Contributors	179

Introduction
Shinjuku and the Kabukichō District

THE CAPITAL OF THE Tokugawa shoguns was the world's largest city. Its successor, the greater Tokyo area, remains so today—a vast, contiguous conurbation with a population of 37 million, sprawling into three surrounding prefectures at the head of Tokyo Bay.

Prewar Shinjuku was a relative backwater among the city's entertainment districts. The biggest of these could be found around Tokyo Station, just east of the Imperial Palace. But after being napalmed to its foundations in the final, brutal months of the war, Tokyo—indeed, nearly all of urban Japan—had to be rebuilt literally from the ground up.

Japan's people, astonished at their defeat and thoroughly disillusioned by militarism, threw themselves into recovery with wild abandon. Shinjuku's local government announced its recovery plan just four days after the surrender.

As money and once-scarce goods began flowing again, black markets sprang up around the big train stations. Many fell under the control of racketeers and gangsters, both foreign (Chinese and Korean residents of Japan) and domestic (yakuza).

By the early fifties, Tokyo was back on its feet and growing again. Urban sprawl and residential development surged, and as the nation's center of government, commerce, and culture, the city's population exploded. The Japanese worked hard throughout the 1960s, creating an economic powerhouse, and hard-working white-collar workers—salarymen—needed a place to blow off steam. Shinjuku grew into the largest entertainment area in Tokyo, and Kabukichō, to the northeast of the station, became its symbolic heart.

By the postwar boom years of the late 1960s through 1970s, when this novel takes place, the gangsters have mostly moved into the shadows, and prostitution and other illegal activities have been hidden away behind closed (but well-known!) doors, but the Japanese company man still drops by his favorite pub every night to de-stress and drink with his colleagues.

Many of the smaller bars and friendly *mama*-sans of that era are gone now, swallowed by increasingly impersonal urban development, but you can still find little establishments hidden away on back streets, with tipsy men being stuffed into taxis by smiling, kimono-clad women who wave goodbye, turn back to their guests to serve another round, and listen to hopes and fears and life stories until deep into the night.

Partial map of central Tokyo

Shinjuku Station district (c. 1970–80)

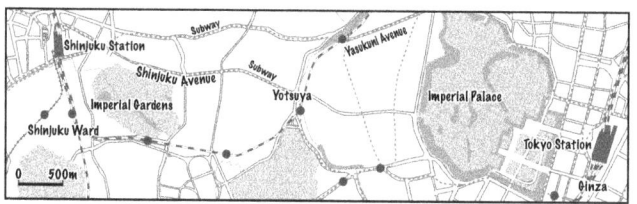

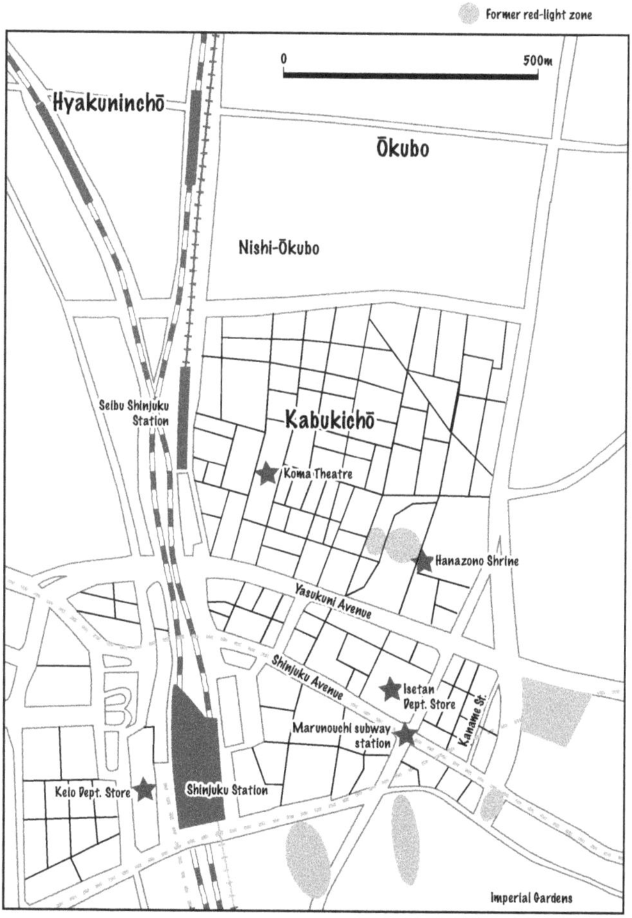

Pushover

SENDA'S APARTMENT WAS TWENTY square yards, floored in wood. There was a tiny corner kitchen, a water heater above the sink, a closet-size toilet and a huge, built-in wardrobe.

It was more than enough for solo living. The furnishings—bed, refrigerator, shelves and dishes, table and rocking chair, threadbare carpet—could've been rounded up from a cheap hotel.

The Yotsuya District Three subway station was around the corner. His second-floor windows looked down on a narrow back street. An architect's office occupied the first floor. Senda had moved in six years ago.

"I can rent you the second floor."

When Nomoto the architect proposed this to him, the space was a conference room. There was no kitchen yet. Half out of politeness Senda had said, "Good. It's fine with me," never dreaming he'd be here six years on. No key money, no deposit, and the rent was a steal, so much so that at first he'd half-wondered when Nomoto was going to kick him out.

Around the time Senda moved in, Nomoto's business took off. The real estate market exploded and his skills were in demand. He moved to a bigger office closer to the huge railway station in Shinjuku, leaving a drafting team on the first floor. Senda wasn't sure exactly what they did. "Tracing"? He wasn't motivated to find out.

After Nomoto renovated the second floor, he filled in the tiny garden behind the building with more apartments. At first the tenants assumed Senda must be related to the landlord. They would come round asking him to unblock a toilet or sign off on a phone installation, thinking he was the super. But Senda and Nomoto weren't relatives, just bartender and customer.

To Senda there was something pathetic about the way his landlord would sit at the counter, always alone, elbows propped, shoulders hunched as if carrying a heavy weight, drinking whisky on the rocks till closing. When he was free, Senda would make small talk, partly to lift the spirits of a blue customer, partly to keep the mood in the bar from sliding. He told silly jokes and gave Nomoto a good-natured hard time.

Nomoto had struck off on his own early, after a rift with his parents. He was hard for Senda to pry open, but once he'd yielded a few personal details, he loosened up completely. They started getting together outside the bar, Nomoto inviting him to play mahjong or springing for dinner.

"You know something? I've been thinking about opening a trendy bar someplace soon. I think you'd be the perfect manager."

Nomoto said it, and Senda counted on it, for a while. Apparently the Nomotos were wealthy, and their son wasn't one for idle talk.

"I got a few people together to fund it. We're raw amateurs. When the time comes we'll leave it to you. It won't happen right away, but I hope you'll do some thinking."

Nomoto seemed serious. He suggested a few basic parameters, and Senda threw himself into it. He sketched floor plans and ran the numbers. His concept impressed the architect, and by the time he'd had been in his new digs half a year, his vision had been transformed into proper blueprints.

But Nomoto's booming business got in the way. Swamped with work and making good money, he seemed to forget his dream of opening a bar. He was out on the town a lot—so Senda heard—but he dropped by The Pot Still, where Senda tended bar, not more than once or twice a year.

"You know, I like this place," Nomoto would say. "I can relax here."

Something in his tone might've been embarrassment over the stillborn plan. He was five years older than Senda. Once the boom came, he'd ridden it quickly to a better lifestyle. He was like a man who'd left home to make good, returning now and then to visit the friend who'd stayed behind in that old wooden building.

Senda didn't begrudge the apparently broken promise. Customers were always talking about their dreams. It was his job to take it all in with a straight face. He could only concede, with that sense of resignation he was becoming heartily sick of, that Nomoto was just another customer.

Once they'd enjoyed bantering like old friends while Senda tended bar. Now Senda treated him with a cautious reserve.

"How long are you planning to stay single?" Nomoto had asked him this the last time they'd met, but Senda got the same question from all kinds of people—customers, hostesses, the liquor dealer stopping by to collect payment.

"I just don't have the time."

He would smile, a complicated smile. That was always his answer. It wasn't surprising. He was thirty-six. For someone his age, working as hard as he did, single life wasn't unusual. And in his line of work, being single was what people more or less expected, even when they weren't forcing him to protest that he was busy.

Marriage. What was the point? In his heart Senda had renounced that future, and every passing year strengthened his resolve.

After ten years and more tending bar, he'd acquired more regular customers than some of the hostesses had. If he moved, his customers went with him. If he forgot to send cards announcing his new gig, they would track him down, demanding to know why he hadn't warned them.

Many of the young salarymen he'd tended bar for when he was just starting out were department heads now. Some were even general managers. Senda was committed to a life in the bar business, but when he thought of the years slipping away as fresh-faced college graduates came into their own, he felt suddenly weary.

So here he was in Shinjuku, managing The Pot Still. He'd been scouted away from another bar four years ago. Yoshiko the Mama was someone's mistress, and The Pot Still was her first go at the business.

At first she'd struck him as having more than a little nerve, inviting him to join her. He'd never heard of someone with zero experience, not even a stack of business cards from customers, succeeding with a bar.

All the responsibility fell on his shoulders, just as though the business was his. Yoshiko had ideas about the way things should be that only a rookie would dream up, and Senda had had it out with her more than once. Later he would realize that he needn't have been so skeptical. Yoshiko had persuaded her "patron" to finance a bar, when and if, and forced him to deliver on that promise. The lease was in her name, and once she had that very expensive and fungible piece of paper, it didn't matter whether the business succeeded with her running it; she'd be set in any case. Senda had taken her half-baked proposals too seriously.

For all that, the business showed a profit quickly. Senda's luck was with him, and he recruited good hostesses. The Pot Still was soon up and running without most of the problems that plague new bars. And once things got going, Yoshiko proved to have a knack for the work. She felt her lack of experience keenly, but turned it to her advantage by placidly deferring to the hostesses. Her imperturbable demeanor added a touch of class.

Now, four years on, she was a veteran, ready to take over if Senda moved on. Whenever he saw her growing independence, he felt his motivation draining away.

The Pot Still didn't belong to him, but he'd worked as though it did, and along the way he'd mentored the Mama. But as the teacher was overtaken by his student, Senda felt somehow he'd been tricked.

It was time to move on. When the chance came—he told himself—he would give his notice. He was ready, though he'd decided nothing, made no plans.

The Pot Still had a dozen hostesses. It wasn't a big room, but the counter near the entrance was small, which made the space seem deeper.

At first there was a piano against the rear wall. Yoshiko had started with the fixed idea that bars had to have pianos. Later Senda replaced it with an Electone. The piano players kept changing, and they weren't always good. The worse they were, the more they pounded the keys, and the green ones answered loud conversation and laughter by pounding even harder. Pianos were also magnets for inebriated customers, but they wouldn't touch the Electone—they couldn't easily sit down and make a conversation-paralyzing mess of "Chopsticks."

Yoshiko came out of an accounting department and needed no help with the books. This at least was a major break for Senda. Having to keep accounts would've meant working half again as hard.

There is no right way to manage a group of hostesses. Senda's strategy was to be a sounding board whenever they wanted to open up. Of course, saying "Let me know if you need advice" wasn't likely to get them to confide in him, but there was something about Senda that seemed to get women talking about their personal lives.

Once he realized he had this talent, he used it deliberately. He couldn't quite explain how it worked, but it was similar to his knack for putting customers in a good mood without doing much specifically.

Night after night he managed the women with understated charm, and sooner or later something trifling would prompt one to confide in him, usually starting with a remark like "I'm so tired. . . ."

Senda's gift was to take these little remarks seriously. The hostesses were dragging a heavy weight called Life. This was how they'd decided to feel. Rather than stroll through Life with a light step, they liked to picture themselves tearfully dragging that heavy weight. It made them feel deep. All Senda had to do was see that weight they were dragging, and let on that he was dragging one too. As soon as the women felt understood, they became fans, as though being understood went both ways. For Senda this seemed slightly strange.

Long before he met Yoshiko, Senda had worked with a hostess named Masae.

She was beautiful, refined, and seemingly educated, but so headstrong that the Mama and Senda had to step in regularly to keep the peace between her and the other hostesses. Back then Senda had an apartment in Hyakuninchō, north of the big rail station. Masae lived close by in an apartment shared with a few other women.

One freezing February dawn he woke to someone pounding on the thin wood of his door. A woman in a loud quilted coat with a black sateen collar stood shivering in the corridor, looking fresh out of bed. In the dimness Senda realized she was a hostess he'd once worked with.

"What's going on?" He motioned for her to come in, but she shook her head.

"Masae works at your place, doesn't she?"

"So?"

"She tried to kill herself. Sucked on a gas pipe. An ambulance took her away. I live next door. I thought you ought to know."

Senda wasn't obliged to rush to Masae's side, but having been told, he thought he'd better go. He dressed quickly.

"I thought she was living with her boyfriend," he said as he and the woman walked back toward Masae's apartment.

"They broke up last fall," she said sadly. A minor dalliance had come to light, and the boyfriend had vanished.

The super at the apartment told him where she'd been taken. Senda walked the short distance alone in the freezing wind to the shabby little hospital in Ōkubo.

The woman next door had smelled gas quickly, and Masae wasn't in any danger. Senda told the nurse they worked together, and she took him to the bedside. As he stood there looking uncertainly down at Masae's sleeping face, the nurse brought him a folding chair.

"Better be good to her now," she said in a low voice, with an edge of hostility. She seemed to think he was the boyfriend.

After the nurse left, one of Masae's hands twitched slightly. Senda sat down and peered steadily at her face. The room was dark; it was hard to make her out.

"Sen-chan . . ." she murmured.

"I'm here." He paused, trying to lighten the mood. "You blew it. Looks like you'll have to keep working."

She started weeping quietly. "It's our anniversary."

"Whose?"

She didn't answer. She just went on weeping.

The hospital let her go the next afternoon. Senda answered a knock and found her outside his door looking pale. He made rice and egg porridge, and she sat on the tatami and ate it slowly.

Masae was from Hagi. Three years ago yesterday, she told Senda, she'd made the long journey east to Tokyo with her boyfriend. The boy was younger than she was, and broke.

"You eloped. That was the anniversary."

"I keep falling in love with weak men," she laughed as she rinsed her bowl in the tiny sink by the door.

The boyfriend had defied his parents to elope with her, but ended up going back home to go to college. On the rebound she'd fallen in love again, eloped again, and been abandoned again.

"Do men always get so homesick? What about you, Sen-chan?"

"I don't have a home to get sick for," Senda laughed.

"You said I'd have to keep working." She sat down on the cushion again and lit a cigarette. Her usually determined expression and voice now seemed weak and forlorn. "You're right. I've got to keep working, don't I?"

Senda didn't answer. She won't be going home for a long while, he thought. Back in small-town Hagi she'd be a fallen woman. She'd take another lover, they'd part ways, and her only option would be to return to Tokyo.

You'll have to keep working.

That was what saved her. She felt understood. From then on Masae was almost painfully easy for Senda to manage. And sure enough, she found another lover. This time the relationship lasted just over a year. But before it ended, she followed Senda when he moved to another bar.

Two Februarys after her attempt, she said to him, "Do you remember what today is?"

It didn't take him long to answer. "It's your anniversary."

"I might try again, you know."

"Better get it over with then," he'd said cuttingly, and after the customers went home he took her out on the town. Finally, without words, they took a room and made love. Masae spent the night weeping quietly.

A week later she brought an older gentleman to the bar and introduced him to Senda. "This is the man I'm going to marry." Senda congratulated the man awkwardly.

"I'm lucky to have her," the man said, seeming embarrassed himself, and they left the bar.

Senda never heard from her again.

HOSTESSES WEREN'T THE ONLY ones looking for understanding. Customers were too, often for personal situations that weren't quite grounded in reality.

The customer with unappreciated talents who never gets a break. The insider who knows all the juicy secrets. The sexpert. The clown addicted to bad puns. All of it at was least partly an act, and each customer wore his day face when the sun was up. A bar like The Pot Still was a refuge where they could assume their favorite personae.

Muroya Hideo—twenty-nine this year—was the only customer who had no bar persona. Naturally this worried Senda.

Muroya was conventional, but no prude. He played mahjong and the horses with reasonable aplomb, yet was somehow naïve for his age. He didn't seem to come from a wealthy background, but he struck Senda as having lived an unusually sheltered life. When Senda asked casually about his family, he learned the father had died early on and recently the mother too.

"Any siblings?"

"Just me."

Muroya answered without noting Senda's interest. Senda could picture the family. The mother would've been the domineering type. Looked at that way, Muroya's feminine aspects came into sharper relief. His choice of topics always smelled of domesticity. Given his age, he almost came across as the head of a household.

There would be money somewhere in the background. A family compound, maybe rental units on the property. The mother would've controlled everything, bent on raising her son to match her image of him. Now she was gone and he was independent for the first time in his life. A bachelor without rent to pay and money coming in would have a good deal of freedom. He could cruise the bars, and every night he made an appearance at The Pot Still. His mother's restrictions had never allowed him to test himself. Now he reacted to the lack of those restrictions by roaming aimlessly through the Shinjuku night scene.

That was how Senda sized him up. Something about this young man made Senda fear for his future, and he handled him with kid gloves. In return, Muroya developed a certain dependence on the bartender.

"Since when did you become Muro-chan's mother?"

One of the hostesses, a war horse twenty years in Shinjuku, enjoyed ragging Senda. She was a veteran before he'd ever stood behind a counter, and she'd watched him learn the ropes. When he moved to The Pot Still, he'd begged her to come along, saying he needed her to watch his back.

All these years she'd been socking it away, and rumors that she'd soon be opening her own place were a decade old, but she was still a hostess. Makeup liked her face, and she seemed to have the knack; her looks hadn't changed in all the years Senda had known her.

One long-ago early summer evening—Senda wasn't sure how many years it was—he'd been getting ready to open up. A woman in a plain linen dress had come through the door and greeted him with the "Good morning" that people in the business used at all hours of the day and night. He didn't recognize her, but she seemed to belong where she was, and he was too busy to pay attention. Ten minutes later she emerged from the changing room, transformed into the familiar War Horse.

That was the first and last time he saw her without her makeup, and even then he'd only had a quick glimpse. If he passed her on the street tomorrow he was sure he wouldn't recognize her. But sometimes he enjoyed teasing her about it. She fed it right back to him.

"Some women never get old, that's all."

Many of the younger hostesses were unrecognizable with makeup, but for the War Horse to get the identical effect for so many years and never show her face without it was a kind of achievement. Still, she'd put on a good deal of weight over that time.

"You pay too much attention to that kid. It's no good," she told Senda one evening, as though the thought had just struck her.

"What, you mean Muro-chan?"

"That boy's got a few loose ones. Pretty soon he's gonna come apart on you."

Senda had to concede this might be true.

The next night, after closing, Muroya dragged him to a coffee shop. As they faced each other across a square table, the young man brought out a small wrapped package and proffered it with a shy expression.

"Here."

"What's this? You're giving me something?"

"Mm-hm."

Senda put the package on his palm and hefted it up and down. "A lighter. Am I right?"

"Yes."

"Well, thanks for that. Let's take a look." He unwrapped the package. "It's a Dunhill. Why would you give me this?"

"Look, just take it, okay? It's a token of gratitude."

"For what?"

"Takako and I are getting married."

Senda stared. Takako was a hostess at The Pot Still.

Then he remembered. One evening about a month back, Muroya had asked for directions to a nearby short-time hotel. The bar was busy and Senda was on his game with the customers. He'd made a few jokes and given him directions to a hotel on the edge of the district.

Senda hadn't seen any dots to connect before or after that interaction, but if Muroya and Takako were a couple, it would've started that night.

"I don't know what to say." He stared absently at the Dunhill.

"It's my thanks to you. Please use it. It's a memento. You'll come to the wedding, won't you?"

"Sure. . . . Look, is Takako on board with this?"

"She accepted my proposal," Muroya said and smiled shyly again.

"You're really getting married?"

"Truly. She said you'd be pleased."

Senda shrugged and lit a cigarette to hide his confusion. When he saw the flame, he realized he'd accepted Muroya's gift.

Senda himself had been working on Takako to get married. He'd been trying to plant the idea in a roundabout way.

"So what if someone says he wants to marry me? What do I do?"

"Marry him, that's what. And soon."

Takako had a sensuous look and a straightforward, uncomplicated temperament, but she also had a flaw: she was incapable of resisting customers' attempts at seduction, though she didn't advertise it.

At first Senda had marked her down as remarkably promiscuous. Yet she rarely took the lead. Instead she would sit quietly until the customer began a conversation. Later in the evening she'd be practically in his lap. When closing time came, they would leave the bar together. It was clear where they were headed.

Some women have a weakness for alcohol. All it takes is a few drinks and they drop their inhibitions. Senda thought Takako might be one of these and started paying close attention to how many rounds she'd had, but he quickly realized that her behavior had nothing to do with alcohol.

Yuriko was the most self-controlled of the hostesses at The Pot Still. Senda asked her for an opinion.

"That girl isn't right." She poked her temple with a finger.

"Not right how?"

"Everyone scores. Try it yourself. If she turns you down I'll give you a ten spot, no questions asked."

"You're kidding. She's a pushover?"

Senda was floored. He'd heard rumors of this species of hostess from his drunken customers, but never imagined one might be working in his bar.

Shinjuku had changed dramatically since the anything-goes era just after the war. Customers who pawed the girls or bluntly propositioned them were few and far between now. Still, men were always tempted to half-jokingly knock on that door. The answer was usually a joke too, and that would be that; but Takako was willing to open the door a bit. Naturally this would provoke the customer to start working on her in earnest.

"You know . . . ? Why not . . . ? Don't you think . . . ?"

Even when Senda could hear only snippets of conversation, the customer's voice and expression were enough for him to know what was under way.

It's a strange fact of the business, but when a customer is trying to seduce one of the hostesses, their table seems suddenly isolated from its surroundings, as if no one else were in the place. Professionals like Senda uniformly disliked such goings-on.

That Takako was so good-natured only made her more pitiable. Pairing her with harmless customers didn't work. There was something about her, like the child other children can't resist bullying, even those who aren't prone to it. She seemed to draw predatory behavior even from the men Senda was sure wouldn't be susceptible.

Once a genteel customer in his early sixties asked Senda to step outside the bar for a moment. "A man my age really ought to know better. I'm sorry, but could you see that Takako gets this?" he said, handing over an envelope fat with cash.

Senda never saw the man again. But word had yet to get around that Takako was easy.

"You ought to hurry up and get married."

In other words, "Move on," Senda said as he handed her the envelope. If word got around, the customers wouldn't leave her alone. As it was, they still thought of her as one hostess among many, and those who scored chalked it up to their charisma.

How must she feel on her way home, those early mornings after a night in a man's arms because of her weakness to pressure? Senda had had too many solitary dawn walks home himself, and he felt anxious when he pictured what Takako must be going through. Still, he'd never suggested she marry Hideo Muroya.

"What do you want, Taka? Muroya's serious about you." He cornered her after his talk with Hideo.

She shrugged. "I'm sorry for the fuss."

"No need for that. I think he'd make a good partner, if marriage is what you want. But you'll have to quit."

"Yes, you're right." She nodded earnestly.

That evening she left the bar with another customer. Senda had to get across to Hideo that she shouldn't be working, but that would mean explaining why. He was torn. The situation seemed to offer no easy solution.

"How are things going, Kozue? Settling in all right?" Senda asked.

Kozue, a young hostess, was waiting for him to fill a drink order for her table. There were three groups of customers in the bar. A keyboardist was playing the Electone.

"Yes, thanks to you," she answered with a lively smile. She'd just started working at The Pot Still. To Senda's veteran eye, she seemed innocent, even immature among the other hostesses, who'd accumulated their share of bitter experience with men.

"Keeping up with your practice?"

"Yes, still at it." She nodded, grateful for the interest, and headed back to her table with a pair of whisky and waters.

"She's nice," Maeda the bartender said to Senda.

"Don't be stupid. She's out of your league." Senda gave

him a sharp glance. Kozue was training with a modern ballet company. Her family wasn't well-off, apparently, and the lessons were a stretch.

"She's a real straight arrow," the old regular who introduced her to Senda had said. "Take good care of her." Kozue worked from seven to half past ten, special treatment for a part-timer. While the cost of clothes and rent forced the other hostesses to keep working, Kozue had one purpose—she spent all her money on her lessons. To Senda, she was from a different world.

"Fell for her, haven't you?" The War Horse was giving Senda the usual once-over.

"Fell hard," he shot back, polishing a glass. "She'll be a great ballerina someday."

"As if you know anything about ballet!"

"I don't know ballet, but I know women."

"Better gobble her up quick, or someone will beat you to her."

He shook his head. "She's delicious. Very crunchy. It's the ballet training."

"Come on, knock it off."

"As you command."

The War Horse lifted her broad derrière from the stool and ordered drinks for her table. "Make mine weak. My stomach isn't so good these days."

One of the hostesses picked up a mic and started singing. She was slender and a bit plain. Apparently she'd once had an artist deal with a record company.

SIX MONTHS LATER, SENDA had to look for a new keyboard player.

"We're getting married."

The singing hostess and the keyboardist had arrived early. When Senda came in they were waiting expectantly.

"Really? You surprised me this time. When people working here get involved, I notice right away. But I had no idea you were a couple."

The woman poked her fiancé's shoulder playfully. "Of course you didn't. We just got together."

"You're kidding."

"It's a strategic match," the musician said with a smile. "I always wanted to make a career out of the piano, and she wanted to be a singer. I guess it seemed natural to team up."

"But we're changing our strategy," the hostess added.

"Changing it? What are you going to do then?"

"Stand-up."

"What, are you sure?"

"Very. We've got a new angle, comedy with piano and vocal. It should work in clubs, too."

"Interesting. I guess it might. But it sounds ambitious."

"He knows someone pretty talented who could take over."

"Well, if you're quitting, we'll be in the market for someone new."

"He can come in tomorrow."

"Fine, but what's the connection between stand-up comedy and getting married?"

"If I'm not hostessing, we'll only earn half as much at first. But if we're married, I mean . . . I think we'll be able to make it." She gave her fiancé a look that was so amorous it was unsettling.

Entertainers. They have a different kind of guts, Senda thought.

THE NEW KEYBOARD PLAYER worked out well, but Takako was still a source of worry for Senda.

Tonight's customer had his arm across the sofa behind her. To Senda, the sight of Takako nestled close to a man, eyes lowered demurely, had become a fixture of the bar.

Every night she left with someone different. The Pot Still had a fairly large clientele, but it wasn't unlimited. Senda wondered whether Takako might not eventually bed them all.

Muroya kept dropping by, looking increasingly gloomy. Most nights he sat at the bar, had a few drinks in silence, and left.

"Don't you think we should just let her go?" Even Yoshiko was concerned. Now and then she would prod Senda to do something.

"Taka, listen to me. Mama's talking about letting you go. I'd like to see you stay, but I don't know if it's going to work."

Senda and Takako were standing outside the bar. Things were coming to a head, and his tone showed it.

She stood there listening with a lonely look. She wore just a touch of makeup; her fine-grained skin was a point of pride. She furrowed her slender eyebrows and murmured, "It's starting again, I guess."

"What does that mean?"

"It's my fault. It can't be helped . . ."

"Did this happen at your last place?"

"Yes. It did." She looked into his eyes. To Senda's surprise, she was suddenly almost defiant. "The last place and the one before that."

Something was odd. There wasn't a hint of guilt in her tone. Perhaps she *was* being seduced, night after night, by a different customer. But if she was up for it, she was. If she went with each one willingly, guilt would be pointless.

But even if she was no hooker, she was a pushover. She ought to have at least a few regrets.

"You'll end up hurting yourself." Senda couldn't help speaking harshly. But Takako smiled. Her smile grew wider and she started to laugh.

"You've got to say no," he insisted. "If they invite you out, just say no." He thought she was laughing at herself, and he meant to buck her up. But she kept laughing until she said finally, "I *try* to say no. Maybe it doesn't look that way." The amusement in her eyes was like an abyss of female karma.

"You're hopeless." He clicked his tongue in frustration.

"You're a good man, Senda," she said as if wanting to comfort him. "As long as I'm working with you, I think I'll be all right."

"Oh, give me a break." He almost added, *You think I want to work with a pushover?*, but thought better of it.

"So what's happening with you and Muroya? If you settle down, other men won't hit on you. It doesn't have to be Hideo, but don't you think you better grab that ball and chain for your own good?"

"I think he's catching on. He's leaning on me, but I can't tell him the truth," she said in a small voice and averted her eyes. As he studied the rounded shoulders beneath her dress and the white, soft nape of her neck, Senda nearly shouted, "Maybe what you need is *my* ball and chain!" But he stifled himself with a cough.

"You are one strange woman." Still off balance from his near confession, he switched to a distant tone.

Once again their eyes met. Her pupils seemed to open onto a stagnant void. In a moment the void was gone, replaced by that lost, vulnerable look. But Senda would never forget the color of that fleeting darkness. It sent things crawling down his spine.

Was Takako the one being seduced every night? For the first time, he wondered.

Yoshiko stuffed the night's cash and receipts into her handbag. "I'm off, Sen-chan," she said and left the bar. The War Horse was the last hostess left. She turned off the lights in the restroom and said good night. Maeda pulled off his bow tie, slid behind Senda and out under the counter, did one last walk around the darkened tables, checking for smoldering butts, and left without saying good night.

Now it was just Senda and Muroya. A half-empty bottle of beer stood between them. Muroya stared into his glass.

"So? Shall we grab a nightcap?" Senda tried to put some cheer into his voice, though he wasn't in a good mood. *Damn it, why is he always like this?* he thought. The way Muroya sat silently, as though he had something to say but wouldn't say it, grated on him.

Takako had given Muroya the slip on her way out. Senda's instincts told him she'd be meeting the young car salesmen who left just before her. He herded a dejected Muroya outside, turned the key in the top and bottom locks, and headed for a nearby hot pot shop with his customer in tow.

They ordered drinks and food and settled in. Senda took the Dunhill from his pocket and made a show of lighting up with it.

"Still set on getting married?"

"Once a man says he'll do something, he can't go back on it." The young man's face was pale.

"You know, I'm curious. Are you actually in love with her?"

Muroya poured himself a cup of hot sake. "I don't know anymore," he said and downed the steaming liquid.

"Have you talked to her folks about it?"

"Not yet."

"But you've been to her place, right? You've met them?"

"Not yet."

"Then you haven't done anything." Senda was aghast.

"Look, she's not your type." He added in a low tone of finality, "I'd stay away. She's not your ordinary woman."

Muroya stared at him, concern dawning in his eyes. "Who is it? What kind of guy is he?"

"What guy?" Senda stared back.

"Takako's lover. It's not like I'm totally clueless."

Senda laughed. "Muroya-chan—you're lost. You can't be that naïve. And yet you're going to marry her."

Muroya frowned and downed more sake. "Tell me. I won't be surprised, no matter what you say."

"I'll tell you up front, I'm not saying this to hurt you. I've wasted a lot of energy looking after her myself. I defended her too. But I can't do it anymore. At first I thought it would be good if you two got married. I was on her side more than yours, but recently I'm worried about you. Takako doesn't have just one lover."

Muroya started with surprise. "Two . . . ?"

Senda shook his head.

"Three?"

He shook his head again.

"Five . . . Eight . . . Ten? No way!"

"She's a pushover. You know what that means. She doesn't have an off switch. If someone hits on her, she won't say no. I thought women like that were one of those bar stories. An urban legend. But they're real. Takako is one of them."

Muroya started crying. "You can't be serious. It's too cruel."

"Nobody's being cruel. Think back to how it was the first time with her. This isn't easy for me either. But it's the truth. I see it every night. I know better than anyone."

"You follow her? To hotels? I can't believe that."

"I don't have to. I've been doing this for years. I know."

"All right. I'll find out myself."

"Don't be stupid. What good would it do? You'll just end up hurting yourself."

"I'll do it anyway."

"What a pain in the ass. You're going to have to give her up one way or the other. And I didn't tell you all this just so you could go out and tail her."

The hot pot was cooling on the table between them. Senda stared at it absently. It occurred to him that it might be better if Muroya went out and proved it to himself after all.

"All right, okay. Go ahead and tail her. But promise me one thing. Don't lose your head and do something stupid."

"Of course. If she's what you say, I'll forget about her."

"Follow her for the next two or three days and see what goes down."

Muroya nodded. He'd had plenty of sake, but his face was white.

SENDA NEVER KNEW HOW Muroya did his detective work. He stopped showing up at the bar, and Senda didn't phone to check on him. Takako was following her usual routine, but after her exchange with Senda she started leaving alone, after agreeing on a rendezvous. Still, though she tried to be discrete, the preliminaries were plain to everyone. Her manner was casual, but once her customer saw his opening, the look on his face was unmistakable. Hit on her once, and she was sure to follow. She needn't have bothered to leave the bar alone.

As he watched her go, Senda was sure Muroya was out there somewhere, waiting for the truth to hit him between the eyes.

"I'm drunk again, Mr. Manager," Kozue said as she brought an order for another round.

"Stupid—what kind of hostess are you, drinking like that?" Senda was genuinely irritated.

"Now that's a friendly greeting. Obviously he thinks hostesses shouldn't touch alcohol," the War Horse said with a laugh.

"You're in a different class," Senda snapped.

"How so? I'd love to know."

"Just look after her, all right? You're supposed to be her mentor." He started mixing up a hangover cure.

"You know how to make a girl cry. I feel older already." She put her arm around Kozue's shoulders and guided her toward the powder room.

"The old lady has her points, doesn't she?" Maeda said. Senda nodded and stared at the powder room door absently.

All you have to do is say no . . . why don't you say no? He'd been about to say that to Kozue. Then he'd thought of Takako and missed his chance.

Muroya never showed his face in The Pot Still again.

IT WAS TWO MONTHS since Takako had quit. Why she left so abruptly was a mystery, but by that time she must've slept with more than half the customers; it would've been hard to keep going with so many in the know. If Muroya was tailing her, they might well have had a final scene in public.

Spring was coming on. Just as the midday breeze was turning a bit tepid, Senda's landlord showed up unexpectedly in Yotsuya.

"It's been a while," Senda said. "Stopping by for something downstairs?"

Nomoto sat in the big rocking chair and rocked back and forth, looking closely at Senda.

"We've known each other a long time."

"Yes. Nearly ten years."

"Do you remember? I told you once I wanted you to manage a bar for me."

"How could I forget? I was counting on it, to be honest." Senda smiled.

"I wasn't lying."

"Look, it's perfectly fine. Things changed for you in a big way."

"Nothing's changed. It's why I suggested you live here."

This was news to Senda. "I thought you forgot."

"Sorry about that. Things kind of got away from me. But I want to keep my promise, finally. I'm opening a small place in Kabukichō. Only if you run it, of course. Can you leave The Pot Still?"

"When is all this happening?"

"I've got the space. Downstairs, basement floor. Do the interior the way you like. When you're ready, of course. We even had a name, remember? Lui.'"

Senda felt himself tearing up. He turned away to search for something in the cupboard. "You remember, don't you? The plans we made."

The rolled-up plans had yellowed. Nomoto blew the dust off and spread them out.

"These are old. These are very old. Ten years will change a person. You designed this carefully. But if we built this today, no one would come." Nomoto chuckled.

"I know you're busy, but if we're going to do this, let's put our heads together."

"I like that. Let's do it."

"I have a bit saved up. Not much of course."

"No need for that. But get out of this run-down place. Lui will be your bar. We'll be together on it."

Senda went to the window and looked out. "I can't believe it. My first customers are big wheels now. I've been feeling like I was going nowhere. I can't believe this is happening."

"In your line of work, you don't go out and get business. The business comes to you. It must've been hard, doing that all through your twenties and thirties."

Senda turned back to him. "But I'm a bit worried. You must have a lot of connections who could be potential customers. You've built so many relationships the past ten years."

"Worried you can't handle it?" Nomoto laughed. "I guess it's natural to be nervous when it's your place. But you did a great job at The Pot Still. Don't worry. You'll be fine." He stood up and clapped Senda on the shoulder.

OPENING A NEW BAR is always a challenge. Nomoto was handling carpets, wallpaper, furniture and other interior details, but there were a hundred things for Senda to nail down, from glassware and everything needed to stock the bar to customized forms and envelopes and matchbooks.

This time was different, too. In every sense of the word, Lui would be Senda's place. He approached the selection of a single cocktail glass with intense focus. The investors would take their monthly cut, but he'd be buying the bar one piece at a time. Still, the terms of the deal lined up in his favor.

With the design finalized, work started on the interior. Senda was at The Pot Still every night getting Yoshiko and her new manager up to speed with his customers as he waited for Lui to open.

"Listen, you've never met my mother, have you?" Nomoto had dropped by to see how the work was coming along.

"Not yet. You mentioned she lives in Aoyama."

"I'd like you to meet her before we open the place."

He drove Senda to Aoyama. The house was old, with a new annex and a large garden.

"This is far too much space, but my mother lives here alone. It's a waste, really," Nomoto grumbled as he opened the little door set into one side of the big front gate. They changed into slippers in the entry hall and made their way down a sunlit corridor to an imposing reception room.

"There's something I better tell you first," Nomoto said uneasily.

"What's that?"

"I'll never renege on my promise to leave the bar in your hands. I'll stick to our contract. Maybe you thought I forgot about it, but I always planned to do the bar with you. It's why I rented you that apartment. Everything's going according to plan. No need to thank me. None at all.

"But do something for me. Look after my mother. I gave her all the freedom she could want living here on her own, but it's not working out the way I hoped." There were footsteps down the corridor. The door opened.

"Taka . . . ?" Senda raised an eyebrow at Nomoto.

"I don't know how to say this in a way that won't shock you, so I'll just get to it. This is my mother."

"Come on."

"It's true. Takako is my mother." Nomoto's eyes were moist. "She's stopped aging completely. You can't imagine how much of a burden it's been. I left home early and stayed away for years. I lived on that back street in Yotsuya and never saw her."

"How can Takako . . . How can she be your mother?"

"She's almost sixty."

"You're kidding."

"Sixty. She always looked younger than her age. At some point she stopped aging completely. No one knows why. She says she was knocked unconscious during the war when a bomb fell close by. That was the first and last time her life was in danger. Maybe it had an effect on her. But she was thirty-two. She looked older then than she does now."

"She looks at least five years younger than me." Senda was dumbfounded.

"The two of you know each other. Takako the hostess is my mother. I sent her to you. You helped her out. Her youthfulness seems to have something to do with sex, as I think you know. After my father died, my mother . . . Takako discovered this. I don't know why people are obsessed with staying young, but I understand the attraction. It's not just her body. Her mind is young too."

Senda studied her. "So all that . . .?"

"Yes. It was me all along." She smiled sweetly. The sun glowed through the delicate flesh of her ears, edged with downy hair. A young woman. No, a teenager. "I've had a long life. It's not hard to pretend you're being seduced while you do the seducing."

"You could've said no anytime, then!"

She shook her head. "I never wanted to. Once you know what it's like to get older, you know how wonderful it is to be young. You people are strange. Every day you get older. You're closing in little by little on the day you'll die. Yet you carry on with life as if you had all the time in the world. How can you do that? If you could put off that day, if you could taste what that's like, I don't think you'd be so complacent."

"There you have it," Nomoto said. "Please find a place for her at the new bar, even if she is a pushover. It's the only way."

Senda sighed and sank deeply into a huge sofa. "Looks like I don't have a choice. Okay, one pushover for the bar. But she's still Takako, same as when she was at The Pot Still. She's not your mother. Let's forget everything that was said here. Agreed?"

"You're a lifesaver. We'll go with that."

Takako started giggling. "Muroya-chan will be looking for me."

"What happened to him, anyway? He told me he was tailing you."

"He was. He even followed me into a hotel and tried to drag me out. He said he'd marry me and keep me at home and fix my personality. Don't worry. That boy doesn't know a thing."

Senda looked up at her with a shiver of fear.

"They say you're quitting," Senda said. Kozue was sitting at the bar, crying. "What's going on with you? You're drunk every night."

The new manager looked at Senda and nodded with a pained expression.

"And it's closing time. What about your lesson tomorrow?"

"I can't do it," Kozue sobbed. "I'm finished."

"What does that mean? Don't you want to be a ballerina?"

"My body won't do what I tell it to. I got fat. I can't move like I used to."

"Because you drink every night. Isn't ballet like sports? If you don't take care of yourself, you lose your edge."

"It doesn't matter now." She went on weeping. Yoshiko was taking all this in from behind the counter.

"She's pregnant. It's one of our customers," the War Horse whispered to Senda. "Her body's changing. It would affect her ballet right away."

Senda turned away. He got his jacket down and slipped into it. "Well, I'm out of here."

"Good night."

He stepped outside. The moon was glowing through

a cloudy sky. *Kozue. Another lifer in the making*, he thought.

Everyone was getting older. Kozue might fatten up like the War Horse. But no one could live like Takako. With each new dawn, everyone was getting older. To forget, they gathered after sunset to drink alcohol. And what was wrong with that?

He put it out of his mind. His bar would feature a legendary pushover. Instead of worrying, he would make the most of it to bring in customers.

That was the plan, he decided.

The Two of Us

She didn't need to turn on the light to use the sink. The kitchen window faced the neighbor's garden and the moonlight, surprisingly bright, poured through.

Yoshie gargled softly and washed her hands and dried them on a towel. Then, seduced by the moonlight, she slid the window open quietly and looked out. Beyond the tiled roof next door, a four-story building rose like a black cube. The moon floated above it, pinpoint sharp.

She stood there for a while, gazing at the sky, her right arm still stretched out to the window. The night breeze caressed it gently.

She was wearing a simple cotton robe. She'd tied the sash hurriedly when she rose from her futon, and a sleeve had ridden high up on her shoulder, exposing her right arm above the elbow. In the moonlight, her skin had a glow that seemed almost erotic.

A motor gunned, shattering the silence. She frowned and shut the window a bit too forcefully. The aluminum sash closed with a hollow thud.

"Water."

A man's muffled voice. Yoshie took a big tumbler from the cabinet beside the sink, rinsed it under the tap and opened the refrigerator.

The tiny light inside the door cast a glow over the red plastic mat. She filled the glass to the brim and put the carafe back in the refrigerator, closed the door with her free hand and drank a third of the water quickly in the moonlight. She ducked through the half-curtained door into the three-mat room beyond. Her weight on the threshold made the dishes rattle faintly in the little cupboard against the wall.

She spoke softly into the darkness beyond the half-open door to the bedroom. "Turn on the light."

The man grunted. After a moment a soft red glow rose up from the floor. This room was six mats, with bedding laid out along the far wall. The pillows lay under a window that faced the same direction as the one in the kitchen.

She reached behind her, slid the door shut, and crossed to the futon. The man was lying motionless, his face in the pillow, left hand still on the light switch.

"Water," she said.

She half-squatted, half-knelt with her right foot on the floor and her left knee on the bedding. She put the cold glass against his temple as she spoke.

Another groan. He lifted his face slowly and brought his right arm out from under the bedding to grasp the glass, turning his upper body to drink the water in one go. His face was youthful, with a pale complexion and a high-boned nose. He looked sidelong at Yoshie as he drank. His almond eyes were almost feminine.

She took the empty glass and put it next to the ashtray on the wooden server by the pillow. The man twisted smoothly over onto his back to make space for her. She didn't join him right away; she was still half crouched, looking down at him intently.

"What?" The man returned her gaze.

"Nothing." She reached out and stroked his hairline gently.

"Your hands are cold."

Her fingers drifted over his cheek, feeling the whiskers

coming in, and moved slowly along his lower lip. She slipped her index finger between his teeth and touched the softness of his tongue. Her fingertip played up and down, small movements against the tip of his tongue.

He looked up from under at her, mock reproachfully. "You're crazy."

"Am I? Why don't you try it?"

She went on playing with his tongue. He counterattacked by sliding a moist hand along the inside of her thigh. She was naked under the robe. Her flower-patterned panties were crumpled into a ball somewhere deep in the bedding.

She went on teasing the man's tongue. His hand started mimicking those movements in precisely the same rhythm. He had moved on to a different part of her body now, and Yoshie was feeling something new. With the movements of her finger she was showing him what she wanted.

"You're crazy..." This time it was Yoshie. She drew her finger from his mouth, pulled away and slid smoothly into the futon. "You're a cheeky one, aren't you?"

She lay close to him on her side, holding his face in her hands, her breasts mounded between her elbows.

"What's that supposed to mean?"

"You're five years younger, you know." She slipped a knee between his legs.

"Are you kidding? You were showing me what to do."

"Now you can strike out on your own."

"Come on." There was surprise in the man's eyes.

"Do you think we can keep meeting like this? You should move on. There are lots of young ladies out there," she said with a hint of mischief.

"This damn sash..." The man started tugging at it. "Why do you bother?"

She reached down, twisting from side to side, and

worked her way out of the sash. She rolled it up and put it on the floor beside the pillow. As she reached out, her breasts were fully exposed. She glanced down at them, then studied her bedmate with a look that was deeply maternal. "Be a good boy this time. Don't yell."

"Bullshit." The man was piqued.

"Oh, no. You really don't remember?" Her expression turned exultantly salacious. The man put his arms around her slender waist and pulled her breasts against his naked chest.

IN THE MORNING YOSHIE fed him a simple breakfast and sent him off around 9:15. She returned to the dimness of the six-mat room, curtains shut against the daylight, and snuggled back into bed.

That night, her young man had possessed her completely. Their earlier lovemaking had primed her, and the second time he'd proceeded more deliberately. He had learned his lesson well, and his movements had drawn her again and again into the blue haze of ecstasy.

At the moment of release, her vision was always tinged blue. Afterward, she relaxed into deep sleep.

She woke to knocking. The clock above the dressing table showed close to noon.

"Coming!"

She got up and opened the curtains partway. Realizing she was still half-naked under her robe, she hurriedly tied the sash. Before she'd cooked breakfast, she had recovered her panties, buried at the foot of the futon.

She knew who was waiting from the knock. Gathering up the tissues scattered across the tatami, she balled them up and tossed them in the wastebasket by the dresser. She took the paper bag from the pharmacist that she'd left on the red-lacquered dresser and added it to the wastebasket to hide the tissues. As she stepped from the room she turned suddenly around, grabbed the box of tissues off the floor and set it atop the chest of drawers.

"I just got up," she said as she unlocked the door.

A woman of similar height and build stood on the landing, dressed in a black midi skirt and a dark brown blouse open to display some cleavage.

"Overslept." Yoshie went back inside and started folding up the bedding.

"Come on. Get a grip, girl." The woman surveyed the kitchen.

"Did we have an appointment?"

"That's not what I meant. Gaku was here last night, wasn't he?"

Yoshie stuck out her tongue and lifted the bedding into the closet. "You figured it out."

Her visitor came into the room and chuckled awkwardly. "There's nothing to figure out. It's the breakfast leftovers. Do you always make him eat standing up?"

"Not all the time." Yoshie moved a small, low table to the center of the room, set out two cushions, and opened the curtains wide as she smoothed her hair back.

"I guess this morning was special. Open a window, it's skanky in here."

"It is not!" Yoshie opened the heavy sliding window.

"What are you doing in that sexy robe, anyway? Don't you think you're spoiling that boy?" the woman asked playfully. She sat on a cushion with her legs drawn to one side. She put the ashtray on the table, got a pack of Hopes out of her bag, and lit one.

Yoshie went to the kitchen and put a pot-bellied copper kettle on the gas burner. The sparker clicked a few times as she waited for the gas to ignite. "Me and Gaku are just about done."

She came back, picked up the clothes basket on the floor by the chest of drawers, carried it into the curtained three-mat room and took off her robe. She reached into the basket, lifted out a neatly-folded kimono and began dressing quickly.

"Done? Are you breaking up?"

"Yeah. I gave him the general idea last night."

The woman twisted around to look at her. "And I bet he showed you exactly what he thought about that. That's why you were passed out the whole morning."

"Stop it, Kyō-chan." The woman's name was Kyōko. Her apartment was a short walk away.

"Still, you're lucky. My vacancy sign has been out for too long."

"Aren't you the one who said she was done with men?"

"But that's how you always feel. At the time."

Yoshie stood before the vanity and pulled off the gaudy plum-patterned mirror cover. She took a half step back and tightened the sash of her kimono. The rough fabric sang dryly as she cinched it into place around her waist.

"Why don't *you* marry the next one?"

"Forget it." Kyōko stared at her friend's reflection with a raised eyebrow. "I'm only twenty-eight."

They were both twenty-eight. For the past year they'd been running a small bar not far from the west exit of Shinjuku Station. They were the only hostesses. They managed it jointly, which made them both Mamas, and they'd named it The Two of Us. Yoshie wore kimono and had a classic hairstyle; Kyōko dressed in the latest Western fashion. Both women turned heads easily.

"I'm *already* twenty-eight." Yoshie finished dressing. She sat down opposite Kyōko and laughed. "But you'll marry someday, won't you?"

"I don't know. I guess so, maybe." Kyōko lit Yoshie's Hope for her.

"Well, I definitely will, and I'd like to soon."

"Why?"

"Because I'm having a great time. The bar's going great, and I'm not hard up for money. But if I got married, I think I'd find a whole different world of things to enjoy."

"Like being stuck at home?"

"Even that. I'd have children, and they'd be cuter than anything."

"You're the marrying type, Yoshie."

"You'd be a good mother too if you had kids. You'd probably be more into it than me."

Kyōko shrugged. "Let's not spend all morning on this subject. The water's boiling."

In the tiny kitchen, the lid of the kettle was starting its dance.

The Two of Us was a deep, narrow space with room for twelve or thirteen customers. There was a counter with hip-high stools running the length of the room, with a restroom at the end. There were no tables.

A net shelf higher than the customers' heads, a bit like the ones in commuter trains, ran along the wall behind the stools. Customers liked putting their bags up on the netting. It was like drinking in a rail car.

More than one customer had joked, "What about straps for us to hang from?" When the bar was packed, people would stand between the stools to drink. Kyōko and Yoshie started calling them straphangers.

There were straphangers every night. The bar seemed to have caught on, and the bartender, Noguchi, was adept at handling customers despite his youth.

When things were slow, both Mamas would sit with customers. When it was crowded, Kyōko would go behind the bar and Yoshie would stay at the counter until there were no open seats. This was Kyōko's idea. It was better for Yoshie to stay out front, so she wouldn't risk soiling her kimono.

"Are you girls lesbians?"

Drunken customers would often tease them because they seemed so close. Kyōko was boyish, and Yoshie's manner was very feminine. Many of their customers harbored suspicions along these lines that went beyond humor.

The two women had nearly begun such a relationship. Before opening The Two of Us, they had shared an apartment and worked at a bar called The Pot Still on Kaname Street.

Once, when a drunken Yoshie had been weeping over something trifling and Kyōko was consoling her, she'd climbed like a child into Yoshie's bed. At some point they'd fallen asleep in each other's arms, and when they woke in the middle of the night, their bodies responded as if they were in the arms of a lover.

They woke at nearly the same moment, still holding each other, and their lips drew together in a kiss. A strange heat overcame their hesitation, and their tongues thrust deeply. Kyōko's upturned breasts pressed against Yoshie's soft, rounded bust, and they thrust their knees between each other's thighs.

"I need a man," Yoshie sighed, pressing her knee even harder between Kyōko's legs. Kyōko was game to continue, but Yoshie's complaint brought home the absurdity of the situation. She laughed.

"You and me both."

That turned it into a joke. But something lingered, and the encounter ended with a sense that some impulse might start things up again. There was an unspoken intimacy between them that did not go unnoticed by their customers. Yoshie had a young lover, Koizumi Gaku; yet, if Kyōko were to ask, Yoshie assumed she would probably lend him to her. That she hadn't done so already was only because Kyōko hadn't taken the initiative.

Noguchi, the bartender, was in his early twenties, big-boned and muscular and around the same age as Gaku, but he was married and over the moon with his eighteen-months-old son. Working between two beautiful women didn't faze him in the least.

None of the three had any bookkeeping experience, and they were hopeless at the ins and outs of entertainment taxes. But luckily, customers from the local tax office were more than willing to help the helpless Mamas.

Because they knew they were terrible at keeping accounts, they didn't let customers run a tab. Drinks at The Two of Us were a bargain, and every bill was settled in cash.

Launching even a small bar is a costly undertaking. Both women had been saving diligently before becoming friends at The Pot Still, and they split the cost of opening. Though they hadn't needed one, they soon acquired a "patron" in the person of a Mr. Tsunoda.

Tsunoda was a man of some means with snow-white hair and a courtly manner, always well-dressed. He was the owner of an apparel chain based in Shinjuku and the ideal patron for Kyōko and Yoshie.

Drawn by rumors of a new bar with a pair of lovelies, he'd become a regular and a fan of these sensual, sexually ambiguous hostesses. At his initiative they'd come to an agreement: the women would give him special attention, but—by tacit understanding—nothing more, though if they should ever need money he would supply it. So far this half-playful, half-serious arrangement hadn't required him to be a true patron and open his wallet, but the women believed that if either of them needed money, he would comply willingly.

Tsunoda often brought friends to the bar, but Yoshie and Kyōko made a point of calling him "Papa" and treating him as if he were there by himself. His friends would grumble, but they were also entertained. Word got around that Tsunoda was the patron of The Two of Us, and he took pride in it.

"Which one of you is he really 'Papa' to?" his friends would sometimes ask pointedly when he was in the restroom.

"Both of us." Yoshie and Kyōko took care to sound convincing, as if they were giving the questioner a glimpse into some female mystery.

"Two for one? Damn it!" the men would grumble, thoroughly taken in. But there was one customer who saw through the pretense, though he dropped by only occasionally. This was Senda, the manager of The Pot Still.

It was Senda who had introduced Tsunoda to The Two of Us. From time to time, he would bring one of his regulars by for drinks, helping the women build up trade.

"You guys have picked up a lot of business off Tsunoda-san."

Senda mentioned this more than once. With its low prices and small staff, The Two of Us could've been a hangout for students from nearby Waseda University, but with Tsunoda's support it was turning into a high-class establishment. The quality of a bar is set by its customers, not its prices or level of luxury. The Two of Us was becoming a regular stop on the circuit for customers who were used to paying more in fancier settings.

"Just don't let it go to your head," Senda warned them. "As soon as you move into a bigger place and hire more people, the customers will stop coming." Kyōko and Yoshie listened and made the most of what they had.

But a cheap bar doesn't always attract desirable clients. There were young people like Gaku Koizumi and middle-aged, tight-fisted salarymen tired of their lives.

Tsunoda was at the counter again tonight, flanked by other distinguished drinkers. Everyone was imbibing the bar's costliest brandy as if by previous arrangement.

"What happens when Papa wants to exercise his option?" one of Tsunoda's friends asked.

Yoshie glanced demurely at "Papa" and lowered her gaze. "That's private."

"Both of you at once. Right, O-Kyō?" Tsunoda's nicknames for the women were O-Kyō and O-Yoshi.

"Oh, Papa!" Kyōko, behind the bar, squealed with embarrassment.

"But you're the ones who insist—"

She leaned across and clapped a hand over his mouth. "You're always so X-rated."

Yoshie stared at Tsunoda, pouting. Their acting was almost too perfect. The jesting mood evaporated.

"Now stop that. How can I drink my brandy?" Tsunoda drew Kyōko's hand away and turned to Yoshie. "I won't say it again. You'll start crying and I can't handle it," he added, chuckling.

One of the party was a middle-aged woman in an elegant hat. "I must say, the two of you are so pretty." She asked Tsunoda, "Can I borrow them for the show?"

"How'd you like to be fashion models?" he said. "It's a nice side job."

"Oh, please! Put me in front of a bunch of people and my knees start knocking," Yoshie said.

"Me too. I've always hated that kind of thing, ever since I was little." Kyōko added.

The old man next to Tsunoda swirled his brandy and said gravely, "I can't fathom what women are thinking, even at my age. You can take your clothes off in front of a man, but wearing kimono in a room full of people makes your knees weak."

Kyōko laughed loudly. "We've never taken our clothes off," Yoshie declared indignantly.

A young customer shot back, "You're much sexier just as you are. I bet your underclothes are stunning."

"Hey, when did you get a look at them?" Tsunoda feigned panic. The party laughed. On the stool nearest the door, a man in a dark suit sat alone, observing the merrymaking with sidelong glances between tiny sips of cut-price whisky.

Noguchi set another gin fizz in front of the woman with the hat. Its style suggested she was in the fashion and accessories business. He rinsed the shaker, put it behind the counter, slid past Yoshie and approached the customer by the door.

"Shimoyama-san's late tonight."

"Mm. He's got a lot on his plate."

The customer's name was Inoue. Recently he'd been coming in more often, mostly with his friend Shimoyama, who seemed to be in the same line of work. What that was, was unclear, but both men came across as gloomy, and they nursed their whisky and waters for hours. They were the kind of customers you didn't want when the place was full and turning people away.

A BAR MOVES TO its own rhythms. It can go from full to empty in minutes. Then a new customer drops in, and another and another, and soon all the stools are taken again.

Some patterns are hard to explain. The same mutual strangers keep arriving within minutes of each other, night after night. The arrival of one particular customer guarantees that business will be slow that night.

Yoshie and Kyōko dubbed these avatars of the slow

evening "Gods of Poverty." The God of Poverty of the moment was Yamazaki Ei'ichi, and what he did for a living was a mystery.

It was Kyōko who'd persuaded him to reveal his first name. Like the image of sharpness evoked by the Chinese character *ei*, he was a man with a knife-like keenness beneath the surface. Tall, with the craggy features of a European, muscular and trim, he wore expensive suits with a practiced casualness. He could be chatty when the mood struck him, but when he stared silently at the counter in front of him, he radiated an icy menace.

"Yamazaki-san's coming tonight."

Sometimes a bar is empty all evening. Whenever it was starting to look like one of those evenings, one of the Mamas would make this prediction.

"That guy's bad luck," Noguchi would say, but the women didn't mind it when Yamazaki was there. In fact they looked forward to seeing him.

"He's attractive, isn't he?" Kyōko was the first to declare this.

"I wouldn't mind being with him," Yoshie confessed on another night. They were both starting to fall for Yamazaki Ei'ichi.

But one evening, when Senda had brought them another one of his valued customers from The Pot Still, he waved them over and whispered, "Do you have a customer named Yamazaki?"

"Tall?"

"That's the one. Sharp dresser, thirty-six or seven, not real friendly."

"I wouldn't say that." Yoshie took exception to this last comment.

"Hold on—don't tell me you're falling for him. I got this from a reliable source. He's a professional."

"Professional what?" Kyōko looked at him curiously.

"Hit man."

"That's impossible!"

"Look, I'm not in a position to know. But one of the mob heavies says he saw him come in here. He wanted me to know."

"The mob? You mean Masakawa and those guys?"

"Yeah. I know it's hard to believe. But your place is getting some traction. I don't want you getting caught up in something you'll regret."

The women exchanged astonished glances.

So it was that several days later, when Yoshie took the call from Tsunoda, who'd left minutes before, and heard that the two men who always sat at the end of the bar were plainclothes detectives, she started shaking with fear.

"Kyō-chan, we need to talk."

It was a slow night. Kyōko was sitting at the bar with Inoue, who was the only customer.

"What . . .?" Kyōko glanced over, but something in her partner's expression prompted her to slip off the stool and walk over with the short, quick steps that always showed her legs to good effect. "What's going on? Is something wrong?"

Yoshie motioned her to face the telephone on the wall. "Inoue is a cop," she whispered.

"When did you hear that?"

"Just now, from Papa."

"That was Papa on the phone?" Kyōko whispered back.

"He comes in a lot these days. Papa says he's waiting to catch someone."

"Does that mean Shimoyama is his partner?"

"I think so. Don't cops travel in pairs for things like that?"

"Who're they looking for?"

Yoshie nudged her with an elbow. "You know. The God of Poverty."

Kyōko covered her mouth in shock. "No!"

"Remember what Sen-chan said? He was right." Both women had a momentary vision of Yamazaki's icy gaze.

"I hope they don't run into each other here." Kyōko looked anxiously toward the entrance. Almost instantly the door opened, and Shimoyama walked in wearing the standard-issue dark suit.

"Good evening!" both women called out cheerily, hurrying to greet him. "We were waiting for you," Kyōko added.

"This is a surprise. Looks like a slow night," said Shimoyama. He and Inoue usually appeared just as the room was filling up.

"Not really," said Inoue. "Things got pretty lively a bit earlier."

"I don't think we'll have any more customers," Yoshie said. "Please relax and take your time." In other words, don't stay too long.

"Well, I'll just have the one drink. The usual," Shimoyama said as he planted himself next to Inoue and accepted a hot washcloth from Noguchi. "It helps that you don't charge an arm and a leg," he added.

"No hidden fees," Noguchi said.

"Still, poor foot soldiers like us will never be able to touch brandy like that." Inoue gestured toward a bottle behind the bar, the one Tsunoda and his friends had been enjoying earlier.

"It's expensive, that's all. It's not so different from the cheap stuff," Kyōko assured him. Shimoyama's whisky and water arrived, and the two men made a motion of lifting their glasses in a toast.

"By the way," Inoue stared at Kyōko. It was a flat, penetrating gaze, without a hint of warmth. "That company president—Tsunoda? Is he really backing you?"

"Oh, dear. You've been listening to us."

"I haven't been listening. Still, I can't help hearing."

"Do you know Papa?"

"Sure. He has a high profile."

"Why should you care about us and him?"

"I just do." Inoue thrust his chin out as if he were delivering an ultimatum. Kyōko flinched with fear. It occurred to her that she was talking to the law. The thought made her want to dig in her heels. She stared back.

"There's a few things I'm lookin' to find out," Inoue said roughly, but he seemed suddenly unsure.

"Listen, can I ask you something?" Yoshie said with a guileless tone. "Maybe I can guess what line of business you're in."

Shimoyama set his glass down and grinned. "Oh. Really?"

"You both do the same kind of work. I'm right, aren't I?"

Shimoyama's grin twitched into a grimace.

"Am I right?"

"Right," he said. "And what would that be?"

She shook her head serenely. "I really couldn't say."

The men exchanged glances and laughed. "You're quite a character. Beautiful too," said Inoue.

"That's what I often hear, but flattery will get you nowhere."

"Is that so?"

"But it's strange..."

"What's that?"

"Inoue and Shimoyama. Are those your real names?"

Yoshie had been a hostess long enough to sense when something wasn't quite right with the picture.

"Inoue" and "Shimoyama" kept coming in from time to time, but they never seemed to choose a time when Yamazaki was at the counter, and there were no confrontations. Now that they knew he was a wanted man, the women's interest in him redoubled.

They were at Kyōko's apartment, getting ready to leave for the bar. Yoshie was content to put up with the inconvenience of an apartment without a bath, but the more Westernized Kyōko couldn't get along without one. So Yoshie had begun showering almost daily at Kyōko's place, instead of using the public bath.

"You have Gaku, you know." Kyōko had started dropping defensive comments like this whenever Yoshie mentioned an interest in Yamazaki. "I like him too, same as you." The women, one in kimono, one in Western clothes, enjoyed this sparring all the way to the bar.

"Maybe I should mention Gaku next time he's at the counter."

"That's weaselly. You should compete with what you've got. The loser gets Gaku."

"You think I'll lose?"

But every evening was busy. The Mamas were so focused on selling their appeal that they neglected their own needs. Yamazaki always seemed to show up when things were slow, sometimes just before closing, sometimes in the early evening after the bar opened.

"Nice . . .," he would say sometimes as he finished off his first drink.

"What's nice?" Kyōko asked him once as he sat at the counter, flanked by the two ladies.

"The taste of a drink after I finish a job." The word "job" made them start with surprise.

"Oh. So . . . when you come here, it's always after you finish a 'job'?" Yoshie said in a hoarse whisper.

"Yeah. It's gotten to be kind of a custom."

"We're closing soon. Wouldn't you like to take me somewhere?" Kyōko said suddenly, letting Yamazaki feel the pressure of her breasts against his arm.

"Sounds good. Let's go, then."

"Just Kyōko? What about me?" Yoshie wasn't going to accept defeat easily.

The door banged open. The women turned, startled. Gaku Koizumi leaned against the wall, eyes on the floor. It was cold, but he seemed to have lost his coat, and his muffler trailed almost to his waist.

"Gaku-san? What happened?" Noguchi said.

"It's freezing," Yoshie snapped. "Shut the door." Gaku's answer was to slide down and sit on the floor.

"Good grief. You're drunk." Yoshie got off her stool, looking annoyed.

"Yoshie! I just can't make it anymore!" Gaku wailed suddenly, toppling over onto his side. She tried to get him upright again.

"He's her little brother," Kyōko said, throwing Yoshie a life preserver as she took Yamazaki by the arm. He was wearing his sharp face now, peering intently at Gaku.

"Bullshit," he said in a low voice.

Yoshie was struggling to get a limp Gaku onto a bar stool, but he wrapped his arms around her neck and kissed her passionately. Still holding him up, Yoshie shot an accusing glance at Kyōko. "All right, I give up. You win. It's closing time. I'll get him home."

Kyōko had given her a fair chance for redemption; Yoshie would give up her shot at Yamazaki without complaint. "I hate to ask you this," she turned to Noguchi, "but could you take him for me? I'll close up."

Noguchi already had his coat and gloves on. He clapped twice, like a weightlifter warming up, and got a supporting arm around Gaku's shoulders.

"All right, let's go. You can sleep it off at your girl's place."

He winked at Yoshie as he left. Like any good bartender, he knew that sometimes it's best to acknowledge the obvious.

That night Kyōko enjoyed her first man in a long time. Pinned beneath Yamazaki's muscular frame, a shadow of danger looming over him, she spread her long black hair in a halo over the pillow and showed him what it meant to lose control. The tide rolled in until she was nearly undone, and the spasms came so close together it was vexing.

"Stop . . . I'm dying . . ."

Finally she begged for mercy. Without a break she feared she wouldn't survive. But her pleading only spurred him on, and he began to moan with urgency. Sensing his ecstasy, she was struck by the biggest lightning bolt yet, and nearly fainted.

Afterward he was surprisingly tender, holding her as she needed to be held. Enfolded in happiness, she buried her head in his naked chest and sobbed.

"I love you—so much. That was so wonderful, I think I might be pregnant. If I am, I don't care. I'm happy," she said through her tears. He bit her earlobe gently, and another spasm raced through her.

"I love you." His tone was definite. "I have for a long time. Marry me."

Cradled in his arms, completely protected, Kyōko lifted her tear-streaked face. "How can we?"

"Does that mean no?"

She shook her head. "But your job . . ."

"What about it?"

"Don't. You can't hide it anymore."

"Why would I hide it?"

"I didn't want to tell you, but two detectives keep coming in looking for you."

"Two detectives. Looking for me."

"Don't pretend. I know about you. I know what you do." Her vision of love in a dark, forbidden world made her tears even sweeter.

"Tell me then. What do you think I do? Why do you think the police are after me?" he said almost mockingly. He was starting to enjoy her confusion.

"Promise. You won't be angry?"

"Go right ahead." His large hands cupped her breasts.

"Hit . . . man."

"Huh?"

"You're a professional hit man."

For an instant, he squeezed her breasts roughly before releasing them with a laugh. He kept laughing and jumped up finally, went to his suit hanging on the wall, and came back with his business card and wallet. Kyoto took in his nakedness dreamily.

When he showed her his architect's association card and driver's license, she sobbed with joy and clung to him fiercely. He took her again, and loved her until she felt as though her body was scattering to the wind.

"Come by the office. You're welcome anytime."

Yamazaki said this almost as an order as he was going out the door.

THAT SAME NIGHT BROUGHT Yoshie unhappiness that was just as complete. As soon as she switched on the light in her apartment, she had a visit from Inoue and Shimoyama. They left with Gaku after arresting him for a string of office burglaries.

Yet, when Kyōko dropped by the next morning in a merry mood, Yoshie told her the story with surprising calm.

"I'd already decided the next time would be our last. If he hadn't been so drunk, I would've given him the night of his life. But I was ready to break it off. I have no regrets. It's not as if I let him spend money on me. But listen—do you think Sen-chan was lying when he told us Yamazaki was a hit man?"

"Let's call him out for it. Give me the phone."

Kyōko dialed. Senda picked up after one or two rings. She started cross-examining him, but her voice soon lost its energy. She hung up finally with a dazed look.

"What?" Yoshie was mystified.

"That guy . . . He asked Sen-chan to tell us he was a hit man so I'd be interested in him. He knew it would work on me. I'm so pissed. He treated me like a fool. He didn't have to. I would've fallen for him anyway."

"What's the problem? You made it with him last night. He even proposed to you."

"It *was* good. I thought my bones were melting. But he didn't have to trick me."

Kyōko stared searchingly at her lap, as though she was trying to grasp something fleeting before it disappeared.

The Sage of Shinjuku

THE QUESTION OF HOW to celebrate the launch of Senda's bar had become a bone of contention among the ladies.

Senda had a high profile in Shinjuku. More than a few bartenders had trained with him, and many hostesses who'd worked with him had gone on to open their own establishments. Now he would finally have his own place, called Lui.

It's the same in any line of work: a new generation of people enter together. Some go on to succeed, often they share a mentor. Partly by accident, Senda had become a mentor for many in the bar business. They'd worked with him early on, found a stable footing, and were flourishing.

The bickering over Senda's opening started at a tiny bar not far from the west exit of Shinjuku Station. It was run by two hostesses, Yoshie and Kyōko. They had worked alongside Senda at a bar called The Pot Still before pooling their savings to open their own place—named, logically enough, The Two of Us. Senda had been a source of constant support. The name had been his idea. He'd helped them choose glassware, designed their matchboxes, and put them in touch with the liquor dealers and other suppliers they would need to keep the bar going. He even introduced them to regular customers of his own. The women were convinced that the perfect solution for his bar opening would be for Senda's friends in the business to pool their money and get him something spectacular.

They first approached Keiko, the Mama of a bar called 21. She'd been a hostess long before Kyōko and Yoshie got their feet wet, but she and Senda hadn't worked together for years. Still, she welcomed the idea of a joint gift right away.

"That's a good idea. I've been racking my brains about what to give him. It's Senda-san. He'll have thought of every detail, and he knows exactly what he likes and doesn't like."

"I know," said Kyōko. "That's why it seemed better to have everyone chip in so we can get him something really special. It saves him from getting silly gifts too. When we opened, someone gave us a wooden bear from Hokkaido. I mean, really. Maybe if we served salmon snacks or something. But we couldn't just shove it in a closet."

"And we can't put 'No Offerings' on the invitation cards," Yoshie said, trying to be helpful.

"What in the world?" Keiko said. "That's for funerals." The young women looked at each other and giggled.

So 21 was in.

Choosing presents to celebrate a friend's opening could be complicated. The best gifts were practical yet looked good on display. But Senda had sophisticated tastes; unless chosen carefully, the gift might be out of place. Gifts like this from customers could be accepted with thanks, but when the giver was in the business, that was something else. Since Lui was on a basement floor, gifts of floral arrangements would have to be set up inside, and they would be on display for a few days. It made no sense to take up space when people were dropping by for a celebratory drink.

Asking Senda what he wanted would be the simplest

solution, but others were probably doing this already. Being in the business meant you were expected to have a sense of style. Taking gift orders wasn't the best look.

A sense of style was exactly what Kyōko and Yoshie were trying to demonstrate, which is why they'd come up with the idea of a joint gift. This was not the most original strategy, but with Senda there would be more people chipping in than usual. A joint effort was sure to produce something terribly impressive.

Next on their list was the Mama of The Pelican, who had known Senda longer than anyone. She'd been around for so long, everyone just called her Mama.

"That's a wonderful idea. Let's do it. You two are smart."

Mama was an old Shinjuku hand. To her, Yoshie and Kyōko were like children. Her own daughter was helping out at The Pelican, and she wasn't much younger.

Using her connections, Mama widened the circle by inviting old friends. But when Kyōko and Yoshie approached Yoshiko, the Mama of the bar where Senda had worked for years before striking out on his own, they ran into problems.

"Go ahead, do what you like. But it wouldn't be right for me to just chip in. I have to give a gift that comes from The Pot Still."

And that was that. Both women had once worked for Yoshiko, and they weren't in a position to press her. Dejected, they trudged back to The Pelican.

"Yoshiko doesn't want to join."

"But why . . .?" Mama was mystified.

"She says it's her duty to give Sen-chan something directly."

"That woman is so pretentious. What duty? I don't believe it."

She had reason to be livid. Yoshiko had never worked

as a hostess; opening The Pot Still was her first go at the bar business. Before that she'd been a civilian, an office worker. Naturally she couldn't manage things at first, which was why she'd hired Senda. Over time, she'd acquired the know-how to run the bar on her own, and Senda had decided to move on.

Now she was acting as though he were the apprentice, she was his mentor, and he was "graduating" from The Pot Still to his own place. This got under Mama's skin. Yoshiko was a full-fledged Mama herself, but she would never have gotten anywhere without Senda's tireless support.

"This is Sen-chan's fault too. He lets an amateur get away with acting like she's a pro," Mama said with mounting irritation. "Fine. Let's see what she comes up with. I'm sorry, but I'll have to pass on the joint gift. I'd rather go head-to-head with Yoshiko."

"Please—don't do that! We're collecting the money already." The women were on the brink of tears. "If Pelican and Pot Still drop out, it won't be nearly as impressive."

"Now, that's not true. You've still got Yūko in Ginza and Club Love and Golden Bear. You'll be fine."

If the two women had been more seasoned, they would've abandoned the plan and gotten something for Senda themselves. Instead they decided the best move would be to tell everyone what was going on, to drum up sympathy and hopefully escape their dilemma.

But while the hostesses and bartenders they'd recruited responded mostly as they'd hoped, the veterans with their own establishments reacted the way Mama did.

"Who does Yoshiko think she is?" the manager of Club Love said.

"If Pelican is out, we're out too." The Golden Bear bailed as well. The Mama of Club Yūko—a Shinjuku veteran who'd recently moved to Ginza—said, "On second thought, put me down for stirring the pot. It sounds like fun."

"Listen, Yoshie. What do you think?" Kyōko said as she got off the phone with Club Yūko.

"I don't know what to do." Yoshie always wore kimono and had a different kind of beauty, refined and quiet.

"No, I mean about them," Kyōko said, exasperated. "They're acting like we're fools."

"How?"

"We're Mamas too. We've got our own place. It doesn't matter how small the bar is, a Mama is a Mama. This was our idea. Who cares if no one likes the way Yoshiko is acting? Why is everyone pulling out? It's insulting."

"True." Yoshie was the calm, collected type.

"Why don't we just forget it?"

"And do what?"

"Get him something ourselves."

"What about everyone else? We already collected half the money."

"We'll give it back. How did we know this would happen? We're not the ones who ruined the plan. Come on, it's the best way."

Kyōko phoned Keiko, the only one with her own place who was still on board.

"It makes no sense. Why is everyone so prickly? Mama is acting like a child. Yoshiko's a civilian, we all know that. You two should be more careful. It's not fair to Sen-chan. I mean, here he is, opening his first place and everyone's bickering about it."

This hit home with Yoshie. She called The Pelican to try to get Mama to change her mind.

"Well, 21 doesn't know Sen-chan like I do. If you want to share costs and cheap it out, that's your business."

That was her answer. Now it was Yoshie's turn to be incensed. "She says we're cheap."

"See? I told you to forget it," Kyōko said.

"We didn't come up with this idea to save money."

"Well, we can't let them say that. We'll get something really impressive."

IN THE BASEMENT OF a building in Kabukichō, not far from Shinjuku Station, Senda was overseeing the interior work on Lui.

"Can you leave the sink behind the counter until the last minute? I'd like to decide when we put it in."

"Why?" Senda's grizzled contractor set down the length of pipe he was threading.

"The health department's in here tomorrow. The closer to finished everything is, the more they'll find that needs changing."

"No problem. You'll never use it anyway. Forcing you to have a separate sink to wash your hands just makes money for somebody else." A white sink about the size of a large ashtray sat upside down on the counter.

"My, what a lovely place." A stylishly dressed woman in dark brown slacks pushed aside chairs and tables, still wrapped in plastic, as she walked toward them.

"Hi there." Senda gave her a relaxed wave. The contractor looked her over.

"You're the Mama from 21."

"Oh, hello. I haven't seen *you* in a while."

"I'd rather see you in the daytime. When I see you at night, I always end up paying an arm and a leg. I can't stand it. Better to stay away."

"You're terrible. You hardly come to see me. And we're not that expensive."

"You are. Your girls drink like fish, and I'm paying for it. At least they should give me their piss."

"That's awful . . ." She almost doubled over laughing.

"What brings you here in the middle of the day?" Senda glanced at his watch.

"I was in the neighborhood and thought I'd stop by. I wanted to see what you're planning."

"How does it look?"

"Very nice. With this atmosphere you'll take Kojima and his friends away from me. They like this kind of place."

"Kojima? He already gave me something for the opening."

"Really? It's early still."

"You're going to laugh. What do you think? A bottle of Old Parr and a bottle of King of Kings."

"He gave you scotch? What was he thinking?"

"Maybe he wants to see them behind the bar. It's fine with me. He can drink it, and I'll charge him."

They laughed. The contractor frowned. "Nice business you people have. The more I work on places like this, the dumber I feel going to them at night." He went back to threading his pipe.

"Listen, I need to talk to you." Keiko lowered her voice. "Things are getting a little sticky."

"With who?"

"Everyone. The Pot Still and Pelican and Club Love and Golden Bear and Yūko."

"That's everybody."

"And The Two of Us."

"What's the problem?" Senda was worried at first, but after Keiko gave him a quick rundown he laughed.

"Everyone's acting silly. What do they think they're up to?"

"They're dug in."

"Over me? Why bother? They don't get it. I used to be a hired hand and sure, I helped a lot of people, at least a bit. But things are different this time. I have to make a success of this. I don't know what Pelican is thinking.

"Why not just let Yoshiko do what she wants? Lui will be a bigger problem for her than anyone else. People who go to The Pot Still aren't there to see her. They'll start coming here. I've got to survive. I won't be telling them to stick with Yoshiko.

"You see? That's why she doesn't want to go in with everyone else. She wants me to think she's doing me a favor, so I'll go easy on her. Kyōko and Yoshie—they're naïve about this too. If I wanted to I could make sure the only customers they get are students and green salarymen. I mean, what's with everybody?"

"You're right, but shouldn't you do something? If you weren't so popular this wouldn't be happening."

"Well, I thank everyone for that."

"Now that I think about it, you're the one who always helped make sure this kind of thing went smoothly. Those girls are trying to take on too much responsibility."

"Oh well. Let me figure something out. Thanks for the heads up."

Keiko left. That seemed to have been the real reason for her visit.

THAT EVENING, AFTER THE crew left, Senda rendezvoused with a middle-aged man at a tiny counter bar behind Koma Theater.

"That's just like The Pelican," the man laughed after hearing the story from Senda. "But it makes no sense that Club Love would drop out too. Nagai's the manager, not the owner. Going in on it with everyone else saves him money. It's better for the business."

"You can't expect him to do that, though. He acts like it's his bar no matter who hires him. Of course, that's one of his good points," Senda said.

"Mm. You're right, he does have that side to him. But sometimes it holds him back. He'll never be more than a manager. How young does he think he is, I wonder?"

"Anyway, I hope you can help. I can't very well take the lead and organize things, since I'm on the receiving end."

"Sure, I'll take it on. The Pot Still can do its own thing, and you want everyone else on the same page?"

"Right. Yoshiko's scared. I'm not going after her business, but I want her to handle this the way she wants, so she can rest easy."

"All right. The rest of the gang haven't been coming by The Pot Still all that much, so they wanted to do something special for your opening."

"Thanks, this really helps. If you're involved, I won't worry. I don't want my friends falling out over me."

"What do you want them to give you? Shall I pitch that too?"

"May as well." Senda started thinking about what sort of gift would work.

That evening the man made his first visit, to The Pelican.

"Why, it's the Sage! It's been a long time. This is a special occasion." Mama was genuinely pleased.

"I've never had a chance to meet your daughter."

"We're honored." She called the girl over. She was just out of university and had an unaffected beauty.

"This is the Sage of Shinjuku," Mama told her. "He's an important man to know." The girl acknowledged him with a dubious expression.

"Well, what do you think of her?" Mama asked, somewhat anxiously.

"Will she be helping out from now on?"

"That depends on her."

"Don't worry. She's perfect for the business. But be careful not to get into any mother-daughter arguments."

"Really? Whatever for?"

"Boss her around too much and she'll push back."

"She's just like me. Very stubborn."

"If you quarrel and she ends up working somewhere else, it'll take her longer to learn the ropes."

The daughter shrugged and turned away. "There, you see?" the Sage said. "She only gets away with that because her mother owns the place."

"I'm afraid you're right." Mama watched the girl walk away. "Well now, did you just happen to drop by?"

"Actually no." The Sage smiled. He was fifty-three or fifty-four, tall and trim, with elegant gray hair. He wore a chic ascot under a light brown shirt open at the neck, with matching slacks and a lightweight jacket of darker brown. Smooth, crisp, and immaculate, a man who knew how to enjoy nightlife in style.

"I thought I'd tie up the loose ends for Senda's housewarming."

"Oh, dear." Mama clapped a hand to her mouth. "You've heard. It only just turned into a problem."

"I think you misread Yoshiko on this."

"The Pot Still . . . ?"

"Her customers are Sen-chan's customers."

"Yes, of course." Mama struck her palm. "I didn't even think of that."

"You should pitch in with everyone else."

"I will. Of course—Yoshiko couldn't join us even if she wanted to."

"You know what Yūko's like. If she knows it won't turn into a quarrel, she's better off going in with everyone else."

"She used to rent from you, didn't she? When she was starting out?"

"Tell her for me, if you could. I don't touch anything outside Shinjuku."

"I know. I'll mention your name, that's all she'll need." Mama smiled with pleasure as she waved goodbye outside the bar.

"Who was that?" When she returned, her daughter was waiting expectantly.

"That was the Sage."

"I know, but the sage of what?"

"Shinjuku, dear. He knows everything that goes on, so much that it's scary. But I'm so happy he thinks you're just right for this business."

"I do *not* believe this." The daughter did not seem pleased, but immediately softened her expression as she turned to serve a customer.

Senda's bar opened.

Bars usually open their doors a few days before the date they report to the health department. And bars run by a veterans like Senda, with roots in the local community, often have a gap between the soft and official openings that is even longer.

While soft openings usually mean discounted drinks, bars like Lui mail out simple invitations and keep the cash register locked. In effect, until the official opening, Senda was running a house party. The sign outside was lit, but that didn't mean he was doing business. Green young tax officials were apt to make a fuss about this sort of thing, but it was private hospitality. It was no different from lighting your front porch light and entertaining guests in your own home.

The sign outside was switched on. When evening came, the guests started pouring in.

"Well, well. Congratulations."

A middle-aged man named Tsunoda—he owned a

chain of clothing stores, most of them in Shinjuku—was the first guest of the first day. He arrived with Kyōko and Yoshie in tow, the former in a wine-red party dress, the latter wearing an expensive kimono of figured satin. They were followed by two men in overalls carrying a heavy-looking crate. They set it on the floor and lifted out a large alabaster Bacchus.

"Amazing. Very impressive." Senda looked appropriately wide-eyed. Yoshie and Kyōko swelled with pride. "It's for the bar, from all of us."

"I'm grateful. It's just right for the place." Senda showed the men the spot he had already selected for it. They put Bacchus in his place and set up a tall inscribed panel alongside it before they left.

The panel listed everyone who'd contributed to buying the statue. Senda read it carefully. "This is just about everyone. Who coordinated all this?"

"We did!" said Kyōko, puffing up again with satisfaction, not least because she felt she and Yoshie were finally being recognized as Mamas.

"My girls owe you a lot for your help." Tsunoda was in a good mood. He was, for public consumption, a patron of Yoshie and Kyōko—implying that he was backing them financially and being "compensated" in return—but in fact he was just one customer among many. Still, he played his role to the hilt, the wealthy older man with a beauty on each arm. The look was flattering and kept things lively with his drinking pals.

"We'll be your hostesses for the evening," said Yoshie.

"But what about your place?"

"I had them take a night off," Tsunoda said with more of his usual pride.

"You didn't have to do that," Senda said.

"It's my pleasure. They wouldn't have made much tonight anyway."

Kyōko didn't like that at all. "What do you mean?"

Senda felt a pang of sympathy. Kyōko and Yoshie's bar was on the west side of the station. It was long and narrow, like a rail car, and the only other help was a reliable young man named Noguchi who tended bar. Still, they wanted the same respect as the Mamas at bars like The Pot Still and The Pelican; because Senda knew just how much they did, he also knew how much Tsunoda's jest, within earshot of other Mamas and customers, was likely to hurt their feelings.

The two women were just then facing a dilemma. They'd been happy having their own place, but they were feeling the limits of its size. Still, they weren't ready to run something bigger. That would mean facing some major business hurdles, and Tsunoda might have to become a real sugar daddy for one of them. Not a few women who ran bars ended up as someone's mistress out of a determination to make the business succeed.

In any case, with Kyōko and Yoshie helping out at Lui, The Two of Us would have to shut its doors for the evening. Senda was more grateful for this sacrifice than for the gift they'd given him.

Though the practice was starting to die out, many people in the business still considered it the done thing to bring valued customers to an opening. For new establishments, building up trade was an urgent necessity. Still, these introductions didn't guarantee that a bar would prosper in the long run. Everything depended on the person running things.

Tonight was special. Bartenders brought customers. Bar managers brought customers. Bar Mamas and bar Masters brought customers. Lui was standing room only.

Amid the crush, the Sage put in a casual appearance. His evening had already started somewhere else; his cheeks were slightly flushed.

"I knew it. This place will do well," he said as he found a seat at the bar and scanned the room. The Mamas and Masters, waiting quietly for his verdict, broke into applause.

"Congratulations, Sen-chan!"

"The Sage's stamp of approval."

Not everyone knew who the Sage was. Some of the customers were mystified by this sudden change in the atmosphere.

"Who is that? Some kind of fortune-teller?"

"Oh dear, no," the Golden Bear's stout and imposing Mama was explaining to a customer she'd brought along. "He's like the boss of Shinjuku. He knows everything about its night life, every bar and club in the district. He can predict what kind of bar will succeed and which hostesses will open their own place someday, and his predictions are almost always spot on. He's not a fortune-teller, but he has a discerning eye. And he's been watching Shinjuku grow for a long time. He knows where you can find bars for sale and what you should pay, better than any real estate agent. He can tell whether a bartender is good just by looking at him. He can even look at a street and pick out the bars that will be empty tonight and the ones that'll be busy."

"And he's right?"

"Almost always."

"Really? That's amazing. So he's like a fisherman who can tell how the fish will be running tomorrow and what the sea will be like from the wind and clouds. That's why they call him the Sage of Shinjuku."

In fact, the Sage was the superintendent of a cheap apartment building in Nishi-Ōkubo, a district close by Kabukichō that was crammed with small residences. There were twenty-some rooms on two floors of the wood-frame building, each less than three yards square.

The Sage had lived there as the super since the building went up, soon after the war.

For a long time the rooms were rented by hostesses who worked in the local bars. This was how an apartment super became the Sage of Shinjuku. He was kind to his young tenants, and they called him Uncle and came to depend on him. As he dispensed help and advice, he learned about the business and the bars where his tenants worked. Over time he acquired a deep understanding of the inner workings of that world.

As Shinjuku boomed, some of the women who'd lived in his building went on to open their own bars. Though the Sage himself was not in the business, he was an expert, and he gave these new Mamas advice they found valuable. Slowly he acquired a reputation for unerring instinct, and people started treating him with respect.

His tenants moved frequently. The women—many of them arrived as runaways—introduced friends from back home to the building when they moved on. As he watched them arrive as green hostesses and move out once they'd reached a level of success, the Sage developed an eye, a sense, for which girls would do well in the business and those who would not, those who were right for the way things were done in Shinjuku and those who would never fit in.

This was a precious skill. Managers at some of the bigger cabarets started relying on his judgment when they hired new girls. Naturally they paid for his advice. And his instincts rarely failed. He was truly a sage.

With time he branched out into other areas. He came to understand the strengths and weaknesses of bartenders and bar managers. He could tell from the patterns of foot traffic whether the evening would be busy or slow. It came to the point where people from outside Shinjuku who were looking to open a bar, having heard of him by word of mouth, would ask real estate agents for an introduction. As an apartment super, he had close ties with many realtors. Through these connections he even gained a reputation with local mobsters.

Still, he was a good man. After years of being called Sage, he was skilled at playing the part. He was an expert in Shinjuku-ology and deserved to be addressed as "sensei." But since there were already more than enough senseis out there, the title of Sage marked him for special respect.

SENDA GOT LUI UP and running without a hitch. For someone with his experience, he'd almost waited too long to get his own place. As always, the Sage's judgment was on the mark. But soon there were exceptions too, such as the prediction he'd given Mama at The Pelican.

"I don't know what I'm going to do." Mama had dropped by Lui to complain to Senda.

"What's the problem?"

"It's my daughter. She hates the business."

"Was there trouble with a customer? If that's it, she'll get over it. Everyone has a bad experience or two starting out. You didn't notice anything special?"

Mama shook her head dejectedly. "It's not that. She really hates it."

"No problems with customers at all?"

"No."

"Maybe it's a boyfriend. Somebody strait-laced."

"It's not that either. She says she hated it from the start. Now she can't stand it anymore. She's practically neurotic. The whole thing's ridiculous. My own daughter."

"Well, that makes her pure and innocent. Shouldn't you be happy?"

"But I've been doing this for so long. I'm getting tired. I was going to leave it to her and have fun playing the elder Mama. I'm so disappointed."

"I feel for you. Look, why not find yourself some young guy? That'll perk you up. Motivate you too."

"Please, don't joke." Mama sounded close to tears. "Men? I'd rather chew rawhide."

"Come on, that's a little harsh."

"You probably don't understand, but men are tiring. Chewing on rawhide is fine when you're young." She put a fingertip pensively behind her ear.. "Even the Sage is losing his touch."

"Did you introduce him to your daughter?"

"He said she had a talent for the business. I'm sure I heard him correctly."

"The Sage got it wrong? That's odd."

"I don't know. Shinjuku's different now. And the west side's nothing like it was. That forest of skyscrapers—that's not Shinjuku."

Senda didn't disagree. When he saw the shining new towers rising west of the station, where the reservoir used to be, he felt no connection to the Shinjuku he knew.

"Maybe the Sage's time is over," he said with a wan smile.

A FEW DAYS LATER, Tsunoda dropped by Lui. "You know the Sage of Shinjuku, Sen-chan?"

"Of course."

It was a busy night. Tsunoda had to sit at the end of the bar, next to the cash register. He toyed with a glass of brandy.

"You think he can be trusted?"

"Definitely."

"Interesting. He seems like quite a man. I get the same answer from everyone."

"Why not? He's a good guy."

"No money, I gather."

"No. He manages an apartment building."

"He's asking if I'd like to invest in a place if he runs it."

"No kidding." Senda's eyes widened with surprise.

"Think he's on the level?"

"So he's finally decided to do it."

"Was he planning something?"

"Not that I know of. But people were worrying he might be. 'If the Sage opens his own place, we'll be left in the dust,' things like that. After all, he's the king of Shinjuku."

"But he doesn't have his own stable of customers."

"No. But he has lots of former hostesses in his corner. In our group alone, let's see, Yūko in Ginza, Keiko at 21 . . ."

"What's the connection?"

"They used to rent from him. He helped them make it in the business. They followed his advice, and it worked."

"Interesting."

"I'm impressed that he singled you out. He certainly has the eye."

"Flattery will get you nowhere. Actually, it was Kyōko who approached me. The Sage brought up the idea of opening a place with her. She's over the moon, getting an offer like that. Is an offer from him such a big deal?"

"Of course. Like being told you're the number one Mama in Shinjuku. So? Where's this bar going to be?"

"He says it's still secret."

"He probably found the perfect place."

"Family?"

"He's married. No children. The wife is handicapped."

"How so?"

"Polio, I think. Something like that."

"Women?"

"Haven't heard any rumors."

"Well then. I'm thinking of taking him up on it, actually. My company's got a vacant place in Sankōchō. It's a good location. You know it?"

"I do."

"It would be ideal if we could do it there. But if it's better to follow the Sage's advice, we could do a swap or rent it out and use the money to fund the bar, is what I'm thinking."

"Leave those decisions to him. He's got more connections than any realtor."

"Really? That's what Club Love says too."

"But that means Yoshie will have to manage on her own."

"She's an amazing girl. She said she's all for it, if it means a chance for Kyōko. Yoshie gave her some money right off the bat."

"She's covering Kyōko's end?"

"Yeah. Kyōko spends pretty freely, but Yoshie knows how to sock it away. She's a dependable girl."

Kyōko and Yoshie were like daughters to him. When he mentioned Yoshie, his eyes shone with affection.

THE SAGE WENT INTO action immediately.

He dropped by Lui to thank Senda. "I hear you put in a good word for me with Tsunoda."

"So you're finally opening a place. Go easy on me, okay?"

"Don't be silly. I'll need your support. I'm an amateur in this business," he said modestly. Then he started explaining why he'd chosen Kyōko to run the new bar.

"I need someone with ambition—the kind of ambition that breaks the mold. Kyōko's got it. Fresh, youthful ambition is perfect. Too much ambition is no good. It can sink the business. I'm going to shape Kyōko's ambition into something beautiful and pure. Just watch. We won't make too much when times are good or lose too much when they're bad. It will be the perfect establishment," he added confidently as he left.

Senda gazed at his alabaster Bacchus. "What should I get her for the opening?" he asked the statue.

The days passed. One day Senda heard that Tsunoda's vacant property in Sankōchō had been sold.

"How's everything?" Senda's contractor had stopped by for a drink. "Anything need adjusting?"

"Thanks for asking," Senda said. "So far everything's fine."

"This area's doing good business, but a lot of people are buying into the south side. They say it's the future of Shinjuku."

"I don't know about that, but they're planning to build out the station in that direction."

"So it's true, then. Have to keep your ear to the ground these days. They say the Sage is the one who lit the fuse on the south side."

"Really? He's into a lot these days. He might be more ambitious than anyone."

"Why don't you open a place over there yourself, Sen-chan? The Sage could arrange it. You'd probably grab the best location."

"Don't have the money. I haven't even paid you yet."

"If you partner with him, I wouldn't mind putting up something myself."

"How much?"

"I don't know. Five million yen?"

This was more than Senda would've guessed. As a contractor, the man understood Shinjuku's potential. It was easy to believe that slipstreaming in the Sage's wake would reduce his risk to zero.

Still, Senda didn't consider the idea seriously. Satoko, the Mama of The Golden Bear—she ran the biggest establishment of anyone in Senda's circle—also begged to differ. She was older and more experienced than The Pelican's Mama, and so stout she was almost intimidating.

"The Sage is losing his touch. I think the people around him need a reality check."

For an instant Senda pictured Kyōko and the contractor. "Why do you say that?"

"He gave me his stamp of approval, but . . ."

"New hostesses?"

"That's right. Three of them. Two weren't new at all. They came from a third-rate bar in Ueno. I had to let them go."

"Is that so . . .?" Senda had an odd feeling.

"The third one was lazy and a pushover. Though you've got one of those too, don't you?"

A FEW WEEKS LATER, things took a darker turn.

"Sen-chan . . ." It was Yoshie's tearful voice, calling from The Two of Us.

"What's wrong?"

"I can't find Kyō-chan."

"What? Say that again?"

"She disappeared."

"Without a word?"

"She didn't even tell me." Now she was sobbing.

"Maybe she had to go somewhere. You know—because of her new place."

"But I called the Sage, and they told me he moved away three days ago. He and Kyō-chan are gone."

"Don't worry. He can't manage a bar and his apartments at the same time. That's why he moved."

"But Kyōko started acting strange about ten days ago. I think something might've happened."

"Strange how?"

"Like she was worried about something. I mean really worried. And sometimes she'd get kind of crazy. Ask me if she was no good, things like that."

"I'll find her. Don't worry, just sit tight."

"Listen, Sen-chan?"

"What, there's more?"

"I guess you'd better know. Kyōko and the Sage have a relationship."

"They have *what*?" He felt something crashing down inside. "Is that for real?"

"It has been for a while."

"Like how long?"

"Since a little before she asked Papa for help with the new bar."

"That's bad." Senda started to panic. The Sage was not who he'd seemed at all. In that case, he could be anyone. Maybe even someone no good.

He got off the phone and was pondering what to do next when an ominous-looking trio walked through the door. He greeted the men quickly.

"Good evening. Out on the town tonight?" He recognized them. They were in the same line of "business" though not members of the same group. It was unusual to find them together. One was a senior lieutenant.

"You're tight with the Sage, I hear," the man said. He obviously hadn't come for a drink. He scanned the faces of the customers.

"I wouldn't say we're close, but he's been around a long time. I do see him now and then. Is there a problem?"

"He conned us."

"How?"

"We trusted his rep, and he ripped us off, big time. On a southside deal."

"How much . . . ?"

"Thirty, forty million—each."

Over a hundred million yen. Senda was speechless.

"If that wasn't enough, it was an all-cash deal. We screwed up, but this guy has been in Shinjuku since right after the war. The Sage of Shinjuku. Never lived anywhere else. That's all we knew—we didn't think to doubt him. Only a native could've pulled the wool over our eyes like that, but that's exactly why we're bent out of shape."

"What are you going to do?"

"If we don't find him by tomorrow morning, we go to the law."

The men left, looking ready to kill.

THE SAGE HAD CLEANED Tsunoda out too.

"Ah well. I got a little greedy. The Sage of Shinjuku and all that. I thought it was my chance to strike it big."

Tsunoda took the debacle with his usual dignity. He was ready to write the whole thing off. "But I feel for Kyōko. He used her to get to me. Putting her front and center gave him leverage. Still, he sure seemed like someone who loved Shinjuku."

"Maybe Shinjuku is the problem," Senda said. "Even the smallest bars are run like companies now. That's fine when it comes to taxes, but the person running the bar gets a company mindset. I think the Sage was losing his grip too. His advice was missing the mark. That must've been hard on him. Shinjuku is turning into something he couldn't understand. Maybe he thought he couldn't stick around."

"Anyway, be good to Kyōko when she turns up. I'll have to give her hell, but I want to help her get back on her feet."

"Thanks for that," Senda said instinctively. Something of the old Shinjuku remained, he thought. But Tsunoda's sagging shoulders showed he was crushed inside.

IT WAS ANOTHER SIX months before Senda heard from Kyōko. Two days earlier the police had tracked the Sage to Izu and arrested him. He'd paid a large sum to set his wife up in a nearby nursing home.

Senda told Kyōko to come into the city and meet him at Tokyo Tower. "Sometimes the view from high up is the best medicine," he said when they met.

They took the elevator to the observation deck. Beyond the coin-operated binoculars, Tokyo spread out to the horizon under its perpetual smoggy haze. Senda let Kyōko pour out her story before he spoke.

"It's over. There's nothing you can do. Go talk to Tsunoda—today if you can—and let him beat you up about it. But don't give him the dirty details. Even if you have to lie a little, it's better to let him think a bad guy took advantage of a nice girl, and she got in trouble. Never forget, he's one of your customers. They don't come to your place to see the underside of things. If you want to do it right, make sure you don't destroy his image of you."

She sniffled and daubed at her eyes with her handkerchief two or three times, as if trying to wipe away a mote. Senda reached into his pocket and got out a coin.

"Here, take a look at Shinjuku. No matter how it changes, it's our town." He dropped the coin into one of the binoculars. Kyoto cocked her hips like a model and put her eye to the scope.

Senda suddenly found himself comparing quiet, dependable Yoshie to Kyōko, seemingly strong-willed yet so often in tears. For a moment he pictured himself telling Tsunoda he wanted to marry her; the old man would surely be happy. Just now Senda was feeling an urge to leave single life behind.

"Listen, Kyō-chan . . ."

"Hmm?" She glanced at him.

"Not that it bothers me, but I'm kind of like a repairman, aren't I?"

She gave him a puzzled look, laughed uncertainly, and turned back to the scope.

A Man of Shinjuku

Takiguchi Shūhei had just exited the wicket of Shinjuku District Three subway station when a voice from over his shoulder brought him up short.

"Well, if it isn't Takiguchi-san!" The woman's rising tone suggested she was more than an acquaintance.

He turned and saw he was right. "What a surprise." He grinned. Whenever he smiled, deep lines spread from the corner of each eye. As soon as he woke in the morning he would look at himself in the mirror and grin. Then he would put a finger on the laugh lines, feeling their depth. It was his way of watching himself grow old.

"You haven't changed at all."

The woman was wearing kimono. She gazed at him and sighed. She was middle-aged, though younger than he was. Her figure had lost its shape, and she didn't seem interested in hiding it.

Shūhei stepped away from the stream of people coming through the wicket. The woman was still in the station proper, on the far side of the low barrier.

"You've put on weight," he said, looking her up and down.

She laughed dismissively. "I'm old now."

"You and me both," he conceded.

"Shopping?" she asked, and Shūhei felt something long-lost and tender rising inside. Ten years, twelve, fifteen... he counted on the fingers in his pocket. They would have a lot to tell each other. For years he'd been carrying around the words he wanted to say to her, like a burden. She must have something to say to him, too.

But meeting her unexpectedly like this made the words vanish. Instead, he felt the weight of the years he'd wasted holding them back.

"Just coming from my brother's place. He lives in Hōnanchō now."

"Your younger brother? The college student. I remember. He must be very successful."

"He's doing all right. Anyway, what about you? You look settled down."

"I am." The woman's tone became a bit defiant. "My oldest daughter is in middle school."

"How many . . . ?"

"Two. The other child is in fourth grade. Listen, let's not stand here. Can I join you?"

"You'll waste the fare. Weren't you going somewhere?"

"Please, don't be mean." She smiled and came through the wicket carrying a shopping bag with a department store logo. Shūhei could sense she was savoring the feeling of stepping into the past.

They took the underground passageway to the nearest department store and found seats in the basement coffee shop. The woman looked him over once again.

"You really haven't changed. Just a bit older-looking."

"You know how old I am. I don't look much different because I didn't get fat, that's all."

"You must still be in business."

"Yeah. It's called Dom."

"Someone told me about it. You opened it right afterward."

"I've been there since. I'm a Kaname Street oldie."

He'd been an employee at a busy cabaret when she was one of the hostesses, back in the days when they called them barmaids. Fresh and innocent, she had awakened a passion in him. He'd been serious about marrying her. But after she'd spent the night at his place once too often, her parents had confined her to the house. He had gone to see them, determined to get their blessing, but couldn't even get a hearing. Instead, they had cursed him and called him a low-class bartender. This made him so bitter that half out of spite, he'd talked a bank into giving him a loan far bigger than he could easily repay, and used it to open a bar on Kaname Street, which had a sleazy image at the time. As he struggled to make his payments, his bitterness and the girl he'd lost were soon forgotten.

The pressure to make money acted as a spur, and in time he paid off the loan. He owned not just the bar but the land it stood on. With no rent to pay, he could relax, and Dom was known as a place where you could get drinks for the prices they used to charge in the good old days.

Shūhei glanced at his watch. He was bored. He wanted to get rid of the woman, but she kept prattling on happily, digging up one old memory after another in no particular order, her tongue racing. The barmaid of years ago was back and belied the smell of domesticity that clung to her.

"Anyway, everything's different now," Shūhei said, cutting her short. "Shinjuku itself is different."

"Yes, it is." Something in her voice suggested she'd gotten the point. She downed the last of her coffee, now cold.

"Tell your husband to drop by Dom. He'd be a good customer." He wanted to finish on an up note.

"I'd better not. He's not climbing the ladder at all." This more or less fit with what Shūhei had heard. Apparently the man was not exactly a comer.

"Well, let's get together sometime." He grabbed the check. The woman was ready to go. She looked at her watch and remarked on the time with surprise.

They left the coffee shop. Shūhei took the stairs to the street. It was a few steps to the subway, but he didn't bother to see her off.

Up on the street the sun was setting. As he waited for the light at the crossing outside the department store, he noticed a slender, stunning woman dressed in kimono on the opposite side, at the front of the crowd. He thought of the woman he'd just left and smiled, a faint, bitter smile.

The bitch never asked me, he thought. Whether or not he was married. Maybe she was sure he must be, or maybe she'd made a point of not asking. If so, it was a flat-out insult. He guessed somehow it was the latter and felt a bit angry.

The light changed. Shūhei steered toward the beauty approaching from the opposite side. A closer look and he could see she was in the business. Did she have her own place? He thought it likely. A woman that attractive wouldn't be out this early, dressed to kill, if she were working for someone.

Just a few paces away now, she swept her right arm, tiny bag in hand, across her body and dipped her head and shoulders toward him demurely. Not yet thirty, he guessed.

"Hey . . ." Shūhei acknowledged her lightly. Her kimono was a rich blue with an intricate white pattern. She kept her head bowed, long sleeves swinging, as she hurried past in a flurry of small steps.

Ah, yes. He remembered. The woman's name was Kozue. She was a girlfriend of Nagai-san, the manager of Club Love, a bar not far from Dom. Nagai was a few years older than Shūhei. If memory served, the woman ran a small bar behind Mitsukoshi.

Everyone seemed to have their little affairs going in the background. Shūhei had had his own string of relationships, but recently he'd had nothing to do with women. Somehow he just wasn't interested. He wasn't avoiding marriage; he simply hadn't made good on his opportunities, and he was still single. If she'd asked him whether or not he was married, and he'd had a chance to tell her he was single, what direction might their conversation have taken? He decided it was better she hadn't asked.

He wasn't so old that he had to put up with being alone. There were hostesses and moneyed women who came to Dom regularly, more to see him than to drink his liquor. There weren't many in the business who owned the land under their bars. Those who had to pay rent felt the burden keenly, and they envied Shūhei. And he was single. That was bound to draw attention.

But the way he saw it, he was a bit too well known in Shinjuku. If he got involved with another professional, his visibility could easily get him mixed up in something sticky. Land prices were going out of sight, and he could end up with an offer he couldn't refuse, like letting one of the local "syndicates" take over some of his space rent-free or being forced to swap his property for something less desirable elsewhere.

He'd never had a vision of his future. He'd just wanted his own place, not for any definite reason. He'd loaded up on debt and bought a bar in an out-of-the-way location. At the time, buying the land along with the business wasn't unusual. Then the subway went in and the developers came, and around the time he paid off his loan his property was worth a ridiculous amount of money.

As he walked up the street toward the bar, the liquor wholesaler's truck overtook him, cases of bottles rattling as it passed. It stopped beneath the DOM sign, and a young man went inside.

Shūhei followed him into the dimness of the bar. The driver waved in greeting. The new bartender was perusing the bill intently.

"Hey there. Thanks for stopping by." Shūhei smiled. "Just give us the usual." The man nodded and went outside.

"Bet you can't figure that out," he told the man behind the counter. He looked to be in his mid-thirties, with a fresh buzz cut. The back of his head was almost blue. He handed the bill to Shūhei morosely. The driver lugged in case after heavy case of beer, stacked them on the counter, and took the crates of empties outside.

"You can leave those there till Hamano gets here," Shūhei told the bartender. "Just polish up the shelves, that sort of thing."

He perched on a stool and got out a cigarette. After several more round trips by the driver, Shūhei signed the bill, and the man left.

"Getting used to the place?" Shūhei asked.

"This is my fourth day."

"Got a girlfriend?" The bartender said nothing, just shook his head. "You're never too old to get into the business. I think you should take a real shot at it. The way you treat customers can just be who you are. There's no right way to do it."

The man said nothing. His expression was a bit lonely.

"Anyway you look different with short hair," Shūhei continued. "People won't recognize you for a while. But why would someone with a graduate degree be hiding out? It must be hard."

"I don't have a choice!" The man turned away from the shelf he was polishing and struck the counter with both hands.

"All right, all right," Shūhei said hastily, waving a hand in apology. "Just spare me another lecture. I told you before—I was twenty when the war ended. Before I got drafted, I worked in a steel mill. I finished grade school and that's it. Back then, middle school was five years. A lot of us didn't go. When I got back, everything was ashes. I ended up in Shinjuku and never left. You oughta drop all that ideology crap. You and your pals remind me of how this town was in the black market days. In fact I just ran into a woman I knew back then." He paused. "People get old, man."

The man smiled faintly and went back to polishing the shelf.

"Shū-san, you ought to do something about this place."

Tanaka, one of his old customers, was sitting at the bar.

"I like it this way," Shūhei said with a deadpan look. "Two hundred years from now, tourists will come in buses to see it." He was sitting on a chair at the end of the counter next to the till, toying with a ballpoint pen.

"Your girls are old-fashion too."

"I don't let them do new fashion."

"Why?"

"'Cause I don't want to disappoint my old customers."

"Why?"

"Because they'll quit me. What else?"

"True. But I'd rather not have leftovers."

"You talking about my girls?" Shūhei's eyes opened wide. He stood up, reached across the counter, and gave the man a rap on the shoulder.

"Don't you touch my Papa," one of the hostesses said and took a seat next to him at the bar. Shūhei laughed. "Papa" Tanaka was right. His lineup of hostesses was fairly unimpressive. He had a stubborn disinterest in making the bar popular. For one thing, he didn't want to pay the going rates for hostesses, which were exorbitant. When it came to trends, he liked to remain a spectator.

"What's wrong with leftovers?" the woman said.

The phone rang. The girl who usually worked the till reclaimed her seat and picked up.

"Master, it's Kurume-san." Kurume was a woman who ran a small restaurant on the corner of a side street.

"Be right there." Shūhei put the receiver to his ear and glanced quickly at Hamano, his regular bartender, and the new man. He nodded. "Thanks."

He put the receiver back and motioned the man to duck under the bar as he stepped quickly between him and Hamano. The door opened. Two long-haired youths with gloomy expressions ran their eyes over the room as they came in.

"See? He's not here," one said.

"Who were you looking for?" Hamano asked.

"Forget it." The youths shrugged. One of them flicked aside the curtain over the restroom door and glanced inside on his way out.

"What's going on?" Hamano looked under the counter. The young man was curled into a crouch on the floor.

"Leave him alone. Stay cool," Shūhei said in a quiet, sharp tone. Hamano looked at him with surprise.

"Who were those two?" asked Tanaka, sensing a situation.

"Nothing to worry about," Shūhei said.

"Not from the mob?"

"No. Not the mob."

"Who's the new guy? Friend of theirs?"

"You could say that." Shūhei wanted to change the subject. "Anyway, I don't have to make much out of this place. It's just me, and I don't need much. I've got lots of regulars. I think people charge too much these days. They want to live in a big condo, buy new clothes all the time, wear diamond rings, play golf. They can do that if they want, if they earn it. But they want to build that lifestyle into their prices. It's an insult to customers. I'm surprised people bother with places like that."

Tanaka grinned. Shūhei knew he wasn't fooling anyone with the change of subject. He scratched his head nervously.

"Still young at heart, Shūhei."

"What makes you say that?"

"Look in the mirror. You've got your fire-eating face on."

"Really . . .?"

Tanaka laughed happily. "Drink up. My whisky is your whisky, right?"

"That's what you used to say." Shūhei got a glass and poured himself a shot. "I'm too old to make mistakes," he said and downed it neat.

"Still. Better be careful." Tanaka peered at him steadily.

When Kurume arrived, Shūhei came out from behind the bar. He ordered Cokes from the till girl and they sat down near the entrance.

"What's going on?" she asked. "There must be twenty of them out there, hanging about."

"Thanks for the call. You saved us."

"No need to thank me, but who are they? One of my younger customers says they're students, some kind of extremist faction. I think he's right."

"It's him, actually." Shūhei motioned with his head toward the new bartender, who was standing behind the counter again. "That's they guy they're after."

"Short hair?"

"Right."

"Who is he?"

"O-Maki's son."

Kurume's eyes grew wide. "Her son? He's all grown up."

"Of course. It's been twenty years."

"But why are they looking for him?"

"I'm not sure. Probably some group that broke up into factions. Now they're going after each other. Seems he was the leader of one faction. These guys are practically killing each other. His faction lost. They want to hunt him down."

"What happens if they find him?"

"He says it won't be pretty."

"Will they kill him?"

"Maybe. We tried to hide him, but they figured out where he was pretty quick. He's been staying here for the past two, three days."

Shūhei pointed to the ceiling. There was a small living space on the second floor that had been vacant for years.

"O-Maki's son . . ." Kurume said in an admiring tone. "What are you going to do if they hang around until closing? Should I call the police?"

"They haven't done anything. What d'you expect the cops to do?"

"But you don't want them beating people up after you close. They might know about the second floor too."

"That's right. If they go round the back, they'll see a window up there."

"We have to find a way to get him out of here."

"There's no way unless those guys leave."

"Let's at least do something. O-Maki helped us all way back when. You don't have to take this on by yourself."

"Any good ideas?"

"Let me talk to Club Love. I can't do anything here." Kurume stood up. "Well, I'm off," she said in a louder voice and bustled conspicuously out the door.

Shūhei called the young man over. "Go upstairs.

Douse the lights," he whispered. The man nodded, face pale, and stepped behind the curtain that screened the restroom door. To one side of the door was a mirror; in the opposite wall was an alcove about a yard deep, with shelves for the hostesses to store their bags and coats. A ladder in the shadows on the back wall of the alcove led to the second floor. People never noticed it unless they knew it was there.

The call from Club Love came quickly. "O-Maki's son? Is it true?" It was Nagai.

"That's right," Shūhei said.

"I just got back from taking a look myself. Those guys are serious. They're a skinny bunch, but their eyes are wild. No telling what they might do."

"We'll figure out something."

"Don't be stupid. It won't be that easy. I haven't been to the cemetery this year, but I went and paid my respects last year. O-Maki was like the Red Cross in the old days. Are you really going to take them on by yourself?"

"What've you got in mind? Nothing dangerous, I hope."

"I'll get in touch with Nakanishi and his people. Gangsters have to make a living too." With that Nagai hung up abruptly.

"Looks like we'll have to hunker down here," said Tanaka, still knocking them back and now quite drunk.

"Why?"

"First Kurume, now Nagai. I heard the whole thing. Sounds like the old gang's on the warpath. This's going to be fun." The old man raised both hands above his head several times, as if doing calisthenics on the bar stool.

"You are a reliable pain in the ass," Shūhei said with a grim smile.

At ten o'clock, the radicals were still patrolling the streets. The information about their man's whereabouts must have come from a reliable source.

"I'm sorry." It was Nagai, apologizing on the phone. "Looks like mobsters these days are just salarymen. They won't touch it. They say getting involved would hurt their legitimate business."

"Don't worry about it," Shūhei said. "We're better off not owing them anything."

"Anyway, we still need a plan. I'll see if I can get some advice." Nagai rang off just as suddenly as before.

"Good evening," Hamano said brightly.

"What are *you* doing here?" Shūhei said in a voice loud with surprise. Satoko, a stout woman of about fifty with a regal bearing, walked in trailed by a younger man.

"That's no way to greet a lady." She took a seat at the bar. He companion scanned the room before taking the stool next to her.

"What inspires the Madam of the illustrious Golden Bear to visit a dive like Dom?"

"I miss your face." Satoko smiled.

"Brandy sour for the Madam," Shūhei told the bartender. "And for your friend?"

"Oh please, Shū-chan. Don't get the wrong idea. This is my bartender."

The man scratched his head shyly. "Nice to meet you. Madam asked me to come along."

Shūhei folded his arms across his chest. "Oh, really?"

"Really," Satoko said. "Club Love called," she said, taking out a cigarette. "Quite a lot of excitement, isn't it?"

Shūhei laughed.

"I thought I'd better get one more look at you while you're still in one piece," she added.

"Just be sure to leave before things get hot."

"Where is he?"

Shūhei glanced toward the ceiling.

"You ought to renovate this place. It hasn't changed since you opened."

"I can't match The Golden Bear."

"I don't mean that. You like everything the way it used to be." She took a sip of her drink and let Shūhei see her frown. He took a bottle of Hennessy from the shelf. Hamano watched him with a pained expression as he mixed a fresh drink.

"There you go!" Tanaka exclaimed suddenly. "Shū-chan of Cabaret Giraud! Best bartender in Shinjuku!"

Satoko turned to inspect the old man. "What was your name?"

"You used to be 'Sakura-san,' right?" said Tanaka. "You were at Giraud for a bit, back in the day."

"And you are . . .?"

"Tanaka. You probably don't remember me. Used to sell vinyl. That Tanaka."

Satoko struck her palm. "Tah-san . . . I remember you. Clear vinyl was popular then. For high heels and things like that."

Tanaka waved a hand. "Not any more. I got out of that a long time ago."

"Really? What do you do now?"

"Prepare court filings. Legal documents. Can't afford pricey joints like yours. That's why I'm still fooling around with Shū-san."

"Sorry about that." Shūhei glanced at the ceiling and put the fresh brandy sour in front of Satoko. The door opened and five tipsy men came in noisily, followed by Nagai.

"So this is the place," one remarked loudly.

They took seats around a rear table. Nagai spent a few minutes with them before breaking away to head for the counter.

"You got here fast," he said to Satoko.

"Thanks to you I get to see Shū-chan again. It's been a long time."

Nagai nodded and turned to Shūhei. "Those guys on the street will stick out once it's late and fewer people are around. We'll have to wait them out."

Satoko snorted skeptically. "In Shinjuku the streets empty out at sunrise."

"Come on, it won't take that long."

"Anyway, we've got to keep the place full until this is over with," Shūhei said, trying to head off an argument.

"Why?"

"What do we do if they come in as customers? They could hijack the place."

"Now that you mention it, they could." Satoko turned and looked the room over. "There's room for seven or eight more."

"Those guys are penniless, probably," Nagai said.

"They could order whisky and water," Shūhei replied drily. "Nurse it for hours."

"So that's why you brought those guys? To fill the place up?" Satoko asked.

"Uhm-hm."

"It's not enough. I hear they're killing each other left and right."

"Give me the phone a minute." Nagai took an address book from his pocket.

Satoko's bartender was behind the counter with his coat off. Dom was packed and full of noise.

"I heard you started a sushi shop in Yotsuya, but I didn't know you were back in Shinjuku," Shūhei said happily. He was sitting next to Satoko, who was flanked by the owner of a coffee shop over on the west side of the station.

"Not a good business, coffee shops. Costs a lot to do

the interior, you can't keep good help, and customers sit there for hours without spending much. No good for people like us."

"Redo it as a bar, then."

"How? Not in that building. They won't let me. No entertainment businesses allowed. I don't know how I ended up buying the place."

A hostess from Ginza was sitting to Shūhei's left. She was only three or four years his junior.

"Everyone has his own place now," she said. She looked a little lonely. Years before she'd been the prettiest girl in her circle.

Shūhei put a hand on her shoulder. "Make too much money and you'll pack it on like 'Sakura-san.'"

Satoko laughed. "He's right. Extra-large isn't enough anymore."

"You were always so glamorous," said Ginza.

Tanaka put his head on the counter and kept chanting, "This is great. This is great," like a mantra.

"What does he think is great?" Ginza said.

Nagai said loudly from behind them, "Come sit with us." He was fairly drunk.

"There's no place to sit," Satoko said.

"We should all be together. This is like a reunion."

"You've had too much to drink."

The door opened and another group came in. "Hey there, we were waiting for you." Tanaka lifted his head off the bar, called out to them, took another drink, and put his head down again.

"Sorry we're late," said one of the new arrivals. She made straight for Ginza. "Well, look at you. It's been ages," she said and gave her a hug.

"What've you been up to?"

The woman looked over her shoulder. "Well . . . This is my husband." The man behind her smiled shyly.

"Oh, how nice to meet you."

"We've got a restaurant in Kōenji. He's the chef."

Shūhei got off his stool. "There's a seat open at the end there. Everybody move down." They all moved one stool over, freeing up two spots for the newcomers.

The door opened again. It was the radicals, four or five in a knot at the door, and more on the street outside.

"Sorry, we're full up. Could you come back later?" Shūhei said.

The men at the door stood their ground but looked slightly daunted as they took in the scene. A mocking voice called from the street, "We need a drink."

"I'm real sorry." Shūhei smiled and bowed slightly.

"Come on, let us in," came another voice from behind as the group outside pushed their confederates further into the bar.

"As you can see, we're full." Shūhei blocked them. One of the men turned and called scornfully, "There's no room."

"Just one drink," came the voice from outside.

Suddenly Satoko got off her stool. She ducked around Shūhei, flicked aside the curtain over the restroom door and flashed a lewd grin at the students. They stared at her with a mixture of surprise and embarrassment, like children ambushed by a troll.

"I need to pee," she said in an oily voice and slid past them behind the curtain. Moments later came the sound of the toilet flushing to cover another sound.

"We're full, guys. I'm not kidding."

The men in the front did a resigned about-face and pushed their way back into the street. The room erupted in laughter as the door closed. Satoko emerged from the toilet. "I really had to pee."

"Thank you, thank you!" A drunken Nagai rushed forward and grasped her hand.

"Stop it. I didn't wash up," she said with a flash of embarrassment, and returned to her seat at the bar. Shūhei glanced at his watch. It was half past eleven.

"Kill the sign," he told Hamano.

"Listen everybody," Nagai said, standing behind Satoko. "I had no idea we could get this many people together with a few phone calls."

"You did well, Boy Naga," Tanaka said, using a nickname from the early years.

"Everyone's still alive and kicking." Nagai's eyes were moist.

Someone called from one of the tables. "Don't get weepy on us, now."

"Listen to me. It's like the spirit of O-Maki brought us together. I mean, look at us. Say what you want, but we're all heading into retirement or whatever you call it. I don't think we'll be together again like this. When we're gone, the old Shinjuku will go with us. Maybe tonight is old Shinjuku's last night."

"Maybe you're right," Satoko said.

"We kept on going. We never gave up," said Coffee Shop.

"Most of us quit to get married and have kids," Ginza added. For a moment Shūhei remembered his old flame.

"Well done, everyone," Nagai said and bowed. Half the room applauded. Shūhei locked the door.

"That guy . . ."

It was two o'clock. No one had left yet. Tales of the old days were being told at every table. Shūhei was drunk. Hamano's and Satoko's bartenders were drunk. Empty sushi boxes were stacked everywhere.

"O-Maki's son . . ." Shūhei was sitting cross-legged on the end of the bar in his socks, drinking whisky. "I know why he got mixed up with this student movement stuff."

Everyone looked at him, curious. "Why?" Satoko said.

They all revered O-Maki. A tiny restaurant—more of a chophouse—run by an upright woman who looked after everyone with motherly kindness. O-Maki had loomed large in their lives.

"It was some little thing," Shūhei said. "That's how it always starts. The kid was in middle school. The cop, it was his fault. Shinjuku Station was different back then. You remember that big, blocky building. Brown. The color of a soldier's cap."

"Yes, I remember," Satoko said.

"The big clock over the entrance was always wrong. There was a police box on the left as you went in. Most people using the station walked past it. That's where they collared the kid."

"Why?"

"No reason, really. O-Maki didn't let him hang out at the restaurant. It was a sleazy area. People like us were in and out of there all the time. It was our hangout. Remember? All the guys acted like gangsters. I did, so did everybody. The girls were worse. They dressed like hookers. They wore turbans any time of day, with crimson lipstick and a cigarette drooping from the side of their mouth. It's no wonder O-Maki wouldn't let him hang out there.

"She tells the kid to get money from home, so she can stock the kitchen, and a carton of PX cigarettes. Lucky Strikes, I think. He puts everything in his school bag, the canvas kind you sling over your shoulder. O-Maki's supposed to meet him at the station. But I guess she was late. One of the cops sees the kid loitering there and decides to check him out. He's a studious kid, got his uniform on, it just makes him stick out more.

"I don't know what sort of guy this cop was, but I guess he was no good. He finds the smokes. He finds a lot of cash, more than a kid ought to be carrying around. He probably just wanted to dress him down, but this gets his attention. So he drags the kid into the box and rakes him over the coals with a crowd watching. The kid's scared about the cigarettes. He doesn't want his mother involved. He won't give them his name and address.

"They take him over to detention in Yodobashi, dig out his textbooks, figure out where he goes to school. They call his teacher. That's how O-Maki figures out where he is. By then it's late. The kid's hopping mad. He hasn't done a thing as far as he's concerned. And the cops can't very well hand back that carton of PX cigarettes after making a fuss over it. So they confiscate them, and O-Maki has to answer their questions. It was a pain in the ass. But for the kid the whole thing was a shock. O-Maki told me about it once. Ever since then he's hated cops, hated any kind of authority."

The room was silent.

"Uh-oh. It's like a wake in here," Shūhei said, embarrassed. "But since I've got you all here, there's something I want to ask. Does anybody want to buy this place?"

"Why . . .?" someone called out.

"It's like Nagai said. Time to retire."

"Not yet. But are you serious about selling?"

"Yeah. I saw my brother today. He's got a good opportunity lined up. I know I can rely on him."

"If you're selling, I'll buy." Coffee Shop was ready to deal. "But you could get any number of realtors to help you."

"Can't do that. I wouldn't sell to a complete stranger, and I don't want anything dodgy run out of here. If I sell to one of you guys, I know how you'll handle things."

The Kōenji chef was starting to salivate. "How much do you think . . .?" People started arguing figures.

"Stop!" Satoko called in a cutting voice. Everyone

looked at her, surprised. "If any of you buys this place, I'll never forgive you" For everyone in the room, Satoko was a symbol of bygone days. She glared around at them with her old headstrong intensity.

"What are you saying? Shū-san is a man of Shinjuku. It's tough for him, but we need him in this old dive until the day he dies. He has to stay. We're not letting him skip out on us. Listen everyone—do you really want Shū-san to leave us? Don't tell me this is our last reunion, that's absurd. And don't talk to me about 'old Shinjuku.' Shinjuku is Shinjuku. We built this town. Please, Shū-san, don't say things like that, it's not the real you. What we should do is find you a wife. Someone who knows the business, someone young and pretty."

"You tell 'em," Nagai laughed. "You're the one who had a crush on him, way back." There was a wave of laughter.

"All right," shouted Coffee Shop. "Nobody buys this bar. Where else can we drink for free?"

"I feel so at home here," Ginza said tearfully. "It's just like in the old days."

"That's it!" cried Tanaka, raising his head from the counter. Apparently he hadn't been sleeping after all. "That's why he never fixes anything. He wants to stop time."

He looked around the room as if searching for a long-lost dream.

It was three by the time everyone left. Shūhei was still cross-legged on the empty counter, swaying from side to side.

"Those guys . . . I'm gonna quit this, this fucking Shinjuku . . ."

"Takiguchi-san?" O-Maki's son had climbed down from the second floor. "That was quite a party, wasn't it?"

"They're all great people, the old gang."

"My hat's off to them." He bowed slightly. He had his coat on and a small duffel bag in one hand.

"Yeah, I guess you can't stay here."

"I'd better move on. I don't want to trouble you."

"Got someplace to go?"

"Yes."

"Be careful. Stay healthy."

"Thank you."

"Hey, let me see you off. You must be hungry too. I know this all-night ramen place. Really great." Shūhei climbed down and got his shoes on.

"Now that you mention it, I was dozing a bit up there, but now I'm starving."

"Sorry about that." Shūhei got his coat, draped it over his shoulders, and went outside, weaving slightly. The younger man switched off the lights and followed him.

"Lock up with this." Shūhei handed him the key. The door was set into an alcove a half-step deep. O-Maki's son stood in the darkness of the alcove and started locking the door.

Footsteps pounded toward them from a side street. By the time Shūhei turned around, five or six men were almost on top of him. All of them carried short lengths of pipe.

"Look out!" Shūhei spread his arms to shield his companion, who was half-hidden in the alcove. The men said nothing, just raised their truncheons and attacked. All at once Shūhei was struck in the shoulder, chest and head.

"You assholes!" he shouted. He stepped back and pushed O-Maki's son into a crouch and sat on top of him. The man cowered beneath him. Shūhei offered no resistance as his attackers pounded him with steel. The son was screaming wildly, as much to scare the men away as to bring help. At first Shūhei covered him staunchly with his body, but suddenly everything went dark and quiet.

"Takiguchi-san! Takiguchi-san!" O-Maki's son was rubbing him vigorously. For a moment Shūhei realized how drunk he was. "Are you all right? Don't give up!"

"Did they get to you?"

"Only a little."

"That's good." The void started closing in again. Shūhei lay in a spreading pool of blood that was hidden by the darkness.

"My god, you're bleeding all over the place. We better get an ambulance."

"The police are after you. Get out of here. Don't let that cop get you twice . . ."

Shūhei tried to laugh, but his injuries were far more serious than they looked. His head dropped. He was stretched out on the doorstep of his own bar.

In his final moments he struggled to say, *So I'm going to die in Shinjuku after all.*

But there was no one to hear him.

Night Train

TAKE THE EAST EXIT out of Shinjuku Station and head for Koma Theatre. Don't go as far as the theater. Instead turn right after a short distance, back into the narrow streets. In the basement of one of those close-packed buildings you'll find a bar named Lui, run by a man named Senda, a bartender and bar manager who worked in Shinjuku for close to twenty years before finally getting a place of his own.

It's a fairly big establishment as Shinjuku bars go. If it were bigger, it would be a club. People in the business can disagree about the difference between a *bar* and a *club*. Some tiny establishments insist on calling themselves clubs, and there are cabarets—the biggest night spots, offering liquor and lots of pretty girls to help you drink it—that call themselves clubs as well. Ultimately the word after the name on the sign depends on the management. The distinctions aren't enough to make a fuss over.

Bars, clubs, cabarets. Then there are *salons* and *snacks* and dives with other names, all purveying liquor and companionship of one kind or another. The differences might seem clear at first, but look closer and they start to blur.

"Remember, we're a *club*," the Mama says proudly to her customers, when she means "a quality establishment." And that may be all she means.

Shinjuku after dark is a town where distinctions are up for grabs, and boundaries are marked ambiguously.

"Life must be easy, doing what you do."

Sometimes customers would say this to Senda in a tone of envy. When they did, he never denied it. The more they pictured the night world as a place of ease and pleasure, the more they enjoyed the time they spent there.

"Oh no—tending bar is much tougher than it looks." Only a bartender who doesn't grasp the culture of the world after dark would say that to a customer.

An unending succession of affairs, a free and rootless existence even in middle age, a life that's always chic and stylish. It's a lifestyle we civilians can't emulate. We have partners, we have kids. We have jobs that aren't boring enough to grouse about. Still, what would it be like to be a denizen of the night? It's something we ask ourselves, especially when we hit middle age. Longing for an answer, we drop in to chat with the barman and drink and feel the world get just a little lighter.

But a life after dark is easy to live carelessly. Few have what it takes to put down roots and hang on for years running a place of their own. It takes far more self-control than the average salaryman can muster.

Maybe Senda was just born decent. Whatever the reason, he'd made it this far without major stumbles. Yes, he'd had many more affairs than the average man, and he'd come close to falling off the tightrope a few times, but while most people in the business burned brightly before disappearing from the scene, he played it straight, he was someone you could depend on.

As a young bartender he was tagged as boring. He spent a long time on the bottom rungs as flashier men climbed past him. Yet he had a way of observing thoughtfully as his customers—novelists and artists and ordinary salarymen—made their way through life. Among a certain clientele, it was always "Sen-chan, Sen-chan," and they stayed with him, becoming fans.

As the years passed and he matured into a veteran, he found himself older than many of his customers. People trusted him, and he became the kind of bartender that hostesses and customers turn to for advice on personal problems. Yet he never gave them anything that could be called advice. He just listened carefully. This was enough to satisfy people, even make them grateful.

Today was one of those days. Lui hadn't been open long when a couple came in and stayed until the bar started getting crowded. Senda didn't charge them. After they left, he pondered the bill before drawing a diagonal line through it.

"Hey, boss..." One of his hostesses, arriving late, took a seat at the bar and started inspecting herself in the mirror of her compact, hoping he wouldn't scold her. "Were those people relatives or something?"

Senda smiled ruefully and glanced over at the fortyish piano player who sat facing the keyboard. The man was puffing furiously on a cigarette.

"That was Tanimoto Masaru. The recording artist." As he said "recording artist," Senda closed his eyes and said a wordless prayer.

"Masaru Tanimoto? Is he new? I never heard his name before," the woman said as she alighted from the stool and headed for the powder room. Several other hostesses were already there, inspecting themselves in the mirror and chatting.

Moved by some impulse, Senda left the bar and walked over to the piano player. He put his hand on the man's shoulder. The player, whose name was Izawa, looked tired and dejected.

"How are you?"

"He left without even singing."

"He'd probably think twice when the guy at the keyboard is Izawa Kentarō himself." Not many years ago, Izawa had been a rising composer of ballads with at least two hits to his credit.

The tardy hostess leaned out of the powder room door and called, "Hey Master! Was that *the* Tanimoto Masaru?" Senda gave her a quick nod.

A customer came in, and the women smiled, ready to work. The bartenders stood a bit straighter.

It was the start of another night at the watering hole.

IZAWA WAS PLAYING ONE of his hits. The hostesses stared closely at the little pamphlets with the lyrics and gave it their best shot. Compared to the latest popular music, Izawa's composition was languid and cloying.

> *Out of Ueno and on past Ōmiya,*
> *A night train calls for home.*
> *How foolish I was to bet on Tokyo*
> *That scarlet neon was my undoing*

Lyrics and melody were classic ballad style. Senda had forgotten how poignantly this song limned the experience of country folk trying to succeed in the big city. But tonight it hit him harder than ever.

In the early sixties, dreams of stardom lured a young man to Tokyo from his northern hometown of Tsuruoka. He passed the record company's audition and made his debut with the ballad playing in Senda's bar. *Night Train*, sung by Tanimoto Masaru, had captivated the public twelve years ago. Words by Maeda Akira, music by Izawa Kentarō. It made him a sensation overnight.

Artists in those days could take a more relaxed approach to their art. Tanimoto developed a taste for nightlife and was legendary for hitting the bars all over Tokyo. He was famous, handsome, and welcomed wherever he went. He had his pick of women and didn't hesitate to pluck a few of the young blossoms who helped staff his official fan club. He was young and off the leash, with all the money he could spend. He thought it would go on forever.

Young women were his devoted fans, but the second hit didn't come. He released another single—and a third—but they failed to chart.

Night Train was his claim to fame, but his record company, composer, and lyricist were soon busy with new singers, and Tanimoto Masaru was forgotten.

Touring the local circuits kept him in harness for a while, but the bookings slowly petered out. Now he made the rounds of bars and cabarets in Tokyo, performing for pocket change. *Night Train* was his signature, but it soon lost its charm. He started covering other artists' songs and learned to clown for the audience. It was during this chapter in his life that he met Senda.

Tanimoto Masaru could never forget that brief interval when he'd tasted stardom. With a little money in his pocket, he dropped by Lui now and then. Only there did he seem to find a way back in his mind to those days of fame, however briefly. And it was there that he came under the spell of Senda's steady gaze.

One night he found himself telling Senda what was on his mind. "Am I really out of the game for good? Do you think I could get back to the way things were, just once?"

He was drunk. He gave the bartender an imploring look, as if he suddenly felt the weight of his life bearing down on him. As always, Senda said nothing, but poured him another shot.

"You're right," Tanimoto said. "All I can do now is drink and forget."

Senda nodded gravely. "Forget about it. That's what this is for." That was all he said.

"Yeah, I'm gonna forget. Better start over. The way things are now, I'll end up in the gutter. I'm ready to do anything. All I want is to get back on my feet."

Senda assumed it was the liquor talking, but Tanimoto was serious. A few months later he dropped by the bar again and announced shyly, "I got a job at a printing plant."

Senda was stunned but said nothing. Tanimoto grasped his hand.

"Sen-chan—thank you. Without your advice, I wouldn't have had the nerve to try."

For the first time, Senda let Tanimoto drink on his dime.

Tanimoto Masaru, ex-idol, worked hard to become Tanimoto Masaru, pressman. Ironically, he had one last fan, and she wasn't going to let the idol disappear.

Her name was Masako, and she worked in a little canteen not far from the printing plant. She was almost thirty. No one would've called her pretty, even to be charitable.

"Masako's never been hit on even once." That was how Tanimoto, with a caustic grin, described her to Senda.

Still, she was a strange one. When he visited the canteen, she treated him like royalty. Now and then she'd put on her best dress and wait for him to emerge from his ramshackle dormitory, like a fan outside a star's dressing room. She'd present him with a cheap bouquet of flowers or a little stuffed bear or a wind chime with a clear, tinkling ring.

Stranger still, she was always equipped with her autograph book, and she always got his signature before she left. The only signature in the book was Tanimoto Masaru's.

"You know, Masako wasn't a fan of mine. When I was

riding high, she never waited outside my dressing room. All this started after I went to work in the plant and started eating lunch at her canteen."

To Senda it seemed rather sad. As a face in the crowd, poor, awkward Masako wouldn't have had a chance to catch Tanimoto's eye. Being a fan of a real star was in itself a kind of dream for her.

Then out of nowhere, Tanimoto Masaru, ex-idol, was in her world. Her yearning for the lights of the big city, like a dam bursting, chased the dreary realities of life from her mind. And he seemed to understand her. People at the canteen and the plant got used to their odd relationship. For a time, the two of them played the roles of star and fan without irony.

"The company put on an anniversary party at the plant a couple of weeks ago," Tanimoto was telling Senda the evening he brought Masako to Lui. "We had a drink there, then went with some of the guys to this cheap bar, where we kept drinking.

"Everybody wanted me to sing. They even had a guitar. So I went for it. I was perfect that night. I even surprised myself. Not to brag, but nobody said a word while I was singing. A lot of people at the plant are in from the country, you know? If you do it right, that song can really get to people who are far from home."

As he'd been singing, Masako was delivering food to the bar's back door. Hearing his voice, she peeked into the room and saw the customers and hostesses listening with rapt expressions.

The song ended, and the room rang with applause. They weren't applauding because he was a star, but because his performance had completely convinced them. As Tanimoto told it, he cried. He held the guitar in his arms and kept on sobbing.

The next day Masako visited his dormitory, but this time she brought neither a present nor her autograph book, and she was dressed in her canteen uniform.

"Tanimoto-san, I'm going home tonight." For Masako, home was Tottori, far to the west of Tokyo.

"Why?"

"After I heard you sing, I realized how stupid I've been. I guess that crimson neon was my undoing after all."

She had never spoken to him like this, one person to another. She'd given up her dream of Tokyo. Tanimoto Masaru, ex-idol, had been her last link to that dream.

"He stopped by for one last drink. Now he's on a night train. Goddamn it, it's just like the song!"

Late that evening, Izawa was deep in his cups. Tanimoto was on his way back to Tsuruoka. When he'd heard Masako was heading home, he decided to go home too.

Izawa Kentarō, ex-composer, lately piano player in a bar, had been left behind, undone by the crimson neon of Shinjuku.

The Sheltering Rain

AIDA MANSIONS WAS THE name on building. Perhaps "mansions" was a bit grand, given what it was.

Take Shinjuku Avenue from Yotsuya, walk three-quarters of a mile or so toward Shinjuku, turn right and go a short distance into the back streets. The road narrows as you go and slopes gently downward. If you're not familiar with the area, you'll wonder if it might not dead end.

The whole neighborhood is apartments, mostly wood-frame buildings, with the occasional condominium rising here and there. One of these was Aida Mansions—four stories of reinforced concrete, with poles for hanging laundry up on the roof, which was edged by a chain-link fence. The building was fairly new. From the street, the clutter on the balconies was just starting to give it a lived-in look.

Senda's condo was on the fourth floor. He'd lived all over—in rented digs in Shinjuku, then Yotsuya, and later Ōkubo. Now he finally had his own place, on the site of an old family-owned confection shop in the back streets of Yotsuya. Senda and the shop owner had known each other as bartender and customer for years. He didn't get a break on the price, but he trusted the man who built the building.

Senda had risen from low-ranked bartender to running his own bar. On the day he moved in, the distance he'd come over the years hit him all at once. Sitting on the floor, surrounded by bits of furniture and his few other belongings, he felt almost rooted to the spot.

But he wasn't there for long. His bartenders and hostesses soon arrived in a festive mood to help him move in. Soon his furniture, kitchen gear, and everything else had found their own places without his being consulted.

"It's not very big, is it?"

All the hostesses seemed to agree. Senda comforted himself with the thought that condos that felt spacious after you'd moved in were close to a hundred million yen, and that was far out of his reach. But the hostesses had no mercy; they all proclaimed it cramped.

"For newlyweds, this'd be just right." One of the hostesses was trying out Senda's mattress. "The bed's next to an outside wall. There's a room between the bedroom and the people next door. You can yell all you want and not worry."

"You yell a lot?" a grinning young bartender asked.

"No, I do not," the hostess snapped. "I've got an apartment with students living next door."

"Ah, so you have to stifle yourself."

"Yeah, I . . . Oh, stop it!" She stuck out her tongue and hopped off the bed.

Once everything was in place, the housewarming gifts came out, the sushi arrived, and the beer caps popped. The afternoon flew by, and somehow Senda started to feel the condo was really his.

"So you finally got your own place." The Mama of The Pelican stood on the balcony, taking in the view. She was holding her housewarming gift, a ceramic wall clock. "Just hope an earthquake doesn't hit."

"Earthquake . . . ?" Senda looked at her with surprise.

"They say a big one's coming. It's depressing. If it's like the one in '23, this building is toast. And look at this neighborhood. It'll be a sea of flames. You better run toward Ichigaya. I hope you checked the route. If not, you should. If you can make it to the fire station, you'll be okay. But wait—people might be looting. I wonder if they'll let you in. Maybe they'll run you off with bayonets. You never know."

"I don't think the fire department uses bayonets anymore." Senda had to laugh.

"Oh well, why worry? You've got your own place, and you can't be certain a quake is coming, now can you?" She smiled playfully.

"Come on. Are you here to harass me?"

Mama stepped inside and clapped him on the shoulder. "Men have it so easy. You've got your future ahead of you. Women lose out. I was over the hill when I was your age."

"What about now?"

"I'm leftovers. But don't count me out. I still get my period."

"Is that leftovers too?"

"Look, Sen-chan. Women get old fast. Stop fooling around and get married. Otherwise leftovers is all you'll have."

"In that case, I'll pass."

Nagai, the manager of Club Love, had been in the business longer than Senda. His housewarming gift was a tabletop lighter.

"I've got a relative, a nice young girl. Want to meet her? You need a wife."

"You're arranging my marriage for me?"

"Don't be embarrassed."

"I'm not embarrassed. You're the one who's embarrassed."

"Of course I'm embarrassed. It's hard to bring up."

Nagai was a strange bird. Most people in the business who'd reached his age had long since opened bars of their own. He still worked for a paycheck, but he had a penchant for helping girlfriends start their own bars—without his wife's knowledge, of course. He seemed to have decided that being a hired hand suited him, and he made no distinctions between his personal interests and those of his bar.

Unfortunately that often rubbed the owner of the bar the wrong way, so he went from bar to bar, sincere and conscientious and rarely rewarded for it. He always wore outsized trousers belted at the midriff and a puffy white shirt, like a fifties movie heartthrob.

"About this girl—the thing is, her parents are a problem. The say they'll never let her get involved with someone in the business."

"Then what's there to talk about?"

"I'm telling you, don't worry. You're a serious guy."

"Me . . . ?"

"Well, on the serious side. You don't hang around in bars."

"By the time I close up, everywhere else is closed too. I couldn't even if I wanted to."

"See? That's how serious you are. Anyway, how about it?"

"Not in the cards."

"You refuse?"

"Sorry about that."

"Well, that's a relief."

"Wha—?"

"I just wanted to see if I could change somebody's life. You've got this great place, and chances to get married don't grow on trees. Look, I wanted to see what you'd say, but it doesn't feel right after all. I don't know what I would've done if you'd said yes."

"You never change, do you?" Senda couldn't help laughing.

"It's your fault. You're a permanent single." Nagai stepped into his shoes at the door. He seemed baffled by the whole conversation. "See you. Congratulations," he muttered and left.

HALF A YEAR WENT by. At first, owning his own place was a constant wonder for Senda. But by the time summer arrived, the building's shortcomings were plain: dew on the walls when it was cold and the heater was running, water stains in the corner of the bedroom ceiling when it rained. On the roof he found a large puddle of water above the leak.

The landowner called the contractor immediately, but the man wasn't much help. After careful and repeated measurement, he announced, "Your problem, see, is the roof ain't level. This corner's lower than the rest, that's why you got yourself a puddle." His tone suggested he'd made a major discovery. He went away after troweling the corner of the roof crudely with cement. The repair was so primitive that Senda didn't expect much, but the next time it rained, the problem was—mostly—fixed.

There were other things to dislike about the building. With only four floors, the landowner hadn't bothered to install an elevator. A simple errand like buying cigarettes meant a round trip on the stairs, which quickly became tiresome. His newspaper and mail went to the ground-floor mailbox. He wasn't going to get dressed just to retrieve the paper, so he made the trip in his pajamas. But on cold or rainy days that was tiresome too.

SENDA WOKE AT TEN as usual and headed downstairs in his pajamas to retrieve the paper. The sky was showing signs of rain, and as he opened the door, fat drops started falling in a slow cadence, dotting the gray tile of the roof next door with black spots.

If it rains now, he thought as he walked down the stairs, it should let up by evening. That was good. Rain when people were leaving work could mean a slow night.

Someone had left a tricycle blocking the mailboxes. He shoved it aside with a foot and pulled the morning edition out of the slot and opened it where he stood. He turned toward the stairs, still reading the headlines, but before he put his foot on the first step, the skies opened.

It was a real downpour. He turned away in surprise from his half-open newspaper to watch sheets of water pound the pavement in front of his building.

A woman in kimono was running down the street toward him, holding her handbag over her head to protect her hair. As she sought protection from the rain in front of the building, their eyes met and she smiled ruefully. "It's pouring . . ."

"Hey, aren't you from Tsunaki?" Senda said. The woman was a hostess at a bar run by one of Mama's protégés.

"You're from Lui. I'm sorry, I didn't recognize you."

"It's the pajamas."

The both had to laugh. The woman was dressed in a formal kimono sheathed in dark blue silk gauze.

"Oh, now I remember. You moved, didn't you? So this is your place."

Senda looked down at the woman's feet. Her white tabi slippers were still mostly dry. "You need to get out of this. It won't let up for a while."

"Oh dear. I had no idea it was going to rain."

"Look at that sky. Why not come up till it stops? Better than standing here."

"I'd hate to trouble you. If you have a guest, I'll only be in the way."

"No guests." Senda started up the stairs. The woman followed him automatically.

"It's a mess, mind you. And there's that guy smell," Senda said as he stood in the door, which he'd left open on the way out. He motioned for her to come in.

"This is nice. Very tidy, too. It's like Lui, almost," the woman said as she slipped off her sandals just inside the door. "You like things neat, don't you?"

Senda turned on the air conditioner. "Take a seat someplace. I'll make tea."

"You don't have to."

"I need some. Maybe coffee is better?"

"Let me do it, then," she said and rose from the sofa where she'd just settled. Senda put a can with coffee beans, an Italian coffee mill, and a coffee siphon on the table one by one. The woman opened the can with a practiced hand and smelled the beans.

"They smell wonderful."

She smiled. She was wearing little makeup; there was something innocent about her beauty. "I'll grind them. I love doing it. It's so domestic."

"Go for it." Senda sank into a chair at an angle to the table, crossed his legs and opened the paper. The dry crushing of coffee beans came to him over the top of the page.

"It's Senda-san, isn't it?"

"Yep. Come to think of it, I don't know your name."

"Kuniko."

"Still at Tsunaki?"

"Yes, I'm still there."

"You get good customers."

"Nothing but old men."

"I hear business is good."

"That's true. Our Mama is young, but she works very hard."

Senda chuckled and kept reading.

"I understand she's known you for a long time," Kuniko added. "When she scolds our bartenders, she always tells them to learn from Lui."

"Kazue's good people. She almost needs someone taking care of her. The older customers like that about her." He paused, then: "So she's riding the bartenders. I'm impressed."

"Oh my, I hope I'm not grinding them too fine."

Senda put the paper in his lap. Kuniko was holding the grinder out, drawer open. The aroma of coffee filled the room.

"I'll leave it to you." Senda pulled an ashtray closer and lit a cigarette with Nagai's gift.

The sound of grinding again. Senda found himself staring at Kuniko's left hand holding the grinder on the table. There was a fresh trace of a ring on her second finger, but no rings on either hand.

"What were you doing in the neighborhood? Do you know someone around here?"

"Yes, sort of."

She couldn't have been visiting a customer from the bar. Tsunaki's regulars didn't live in neighborhoods like this. Still, she wasn't dressed for a casual visit. Senda didn't feel like digging deeper.

"Where are you from originally?" he asked.

"Utsunomiya."

"Close to Tokyo."

"Yes."

She poured the ground beans into the upper chamber of the siphon. Senda went back to the paper.

"It just keeps raining." While the water boiled in the siphon, Kuniko stood at the window looking over the neighborhood. She murmured the same thing again.

"Another hour, maybe two," Senda said.

"I'm sorry to come barging in like this."

"Well, take your time. When it stops, it'll stop all at once. We should get a nice sunset tonight."

"Do you think so?"

"The whole sky beyond the tracks will be crimson. Shinjuku gets some nice sunsets."

"Pelican's Mama visited us recently. She was decked out in bright red."

"Yeah, I know the outfit." Senda laughed. The clear water in the lower chamber of the siphon rose quickly through the ground beans. Kuniko sat down again.

"It might be her daughter's influence," Senda said. "Not poking fun, but it does make her look like a bell pepper."

"Or a chili pepper."

"She's fat. I'd go with bell pepper."

They laughed. They drank the coffee and the morning slipped away as they traded stories about customers and people in the business.

Finally the rain stopped. Patches of blue peeked through. Kuniko thanked him and stepped into her sandals.

"The street in front of the tofu shop is probably a lake," Senda said. "If you're headed for the station, better turn left before that."

"You think of everything, Senda-san." She laughed teasingly and stepped out the door.

"Drop by again when it rains. You can always find shelter here."

"Well, goodbye."

Senda put his hand on the doorknob and leaned out into the corridor. Kuniko looked back and smiled as she disappeared down the stairs.

That was how it started.

Next day around six, Kuniko dropped by Lui. A customer named Oketani, who published a magazine covering the bar business in his free time, had just settled in at the counter.

"Good evening." Between people in the business, it was "Good morning," but Kuniko didn't want Oketani to think she was working there.

"Well hello," Senda said from behind the counter. He smiled and raised a hand in greeting. He'd been hoping she'd stop in.

"Thank you for yesterday."

She seemed different from the day before. It was evening now, and her bearing was clearly that of a hostess.

"Did you get around the puddles all right?"

"Not completely." She smiled. "I appreciate your kindness." She dipped her head a bit stiffly. She was wearing kimono again. Her hair was tied up in back and gleamed in the dimness.

"I brought something." She put a small square package on the edge of the counter.

"Hey, no need for that."

"It's coffee beans."

"Really . . ."

"These beans taste a little different, by the way."

"Where are they from?"

"There's a slip inside with all the details."

"Okay. Well, thanks for that."

"See you, then." She turned away.

"Going already? Why don't you take your time?"

"I'm working."

Senda nodded. "See you again." She climbed the stairs to the street.

"Who was that?" Oketani asked.

"Not bad, eh?"

"Beautiful. Sexy."

"Good personality too."

"Senda's stamp of approval. Where does she work?"

"I'm not telling."

"Come on. I'll take a run at her. Say you introduced me."

"That's why I'm not telling."

"How come?"

Senda took a moment to clear his throat. "She was at my place until eleven yesterday morning."

"Well I'll be damned. So you finally decided to settle down?"

"I'm not sure about that."

"Why? You're already with her, aren't you?"

"What makes you so sure?"

"You just told me. She spent the night with you. In Yotsuya, at your place."

"I said she was there until eleven. She came around ten. So I guess she was there about an hour."

"Why, you rascal." Oketani picked up an almond and threw it at him playfully. "But I envy you. I've got a wife."

"What do you mean? You were head over heels. That's why you two got together."

"That's right. 'Got together,' that's a good way to put it. A man and a woman get together . . . Brings up all kinds of images."

"The question is, what gets together with what?"

"This gets together with that. News to you?"

"I know the 'this,' anyway."

"What would that be?"

"My big toe."

"Very funny."

Ishii, the bartender, got down a bottle of Cutty Sark and uncorked it.

"Your boss is a bit immature," Oketani said to him. "A baby."

"I doubt that. I got a look once."

"A look at what?"

"He's packing a lot more than any baby."

"Really? That much, huh?"

"Jealous?"

"Okay, so I'm short."

"Really? I like 'em short," said the hostess who'd just walked in.

"Sen-chan, she insulted me!" Oketani wailed.

It was the start of a typical evening.

Toward closing, Nagai came in with a customer from his bar.

"Minagawa-san," Nagai said, introducing him to Senda. "He's a big wheel in the securities business." The three men took a table with a trio of hostesses, and things got lively. The title on Minagawa's business card was Sales Director.

"Are you out by yourself tonight?" Senda asked.

"Yep. I left the young people at Club Love. They have more fun when I'm not there."

"It's hard to unwind when the boss is around," Nagai put in as he nibbled a whisky and water. His tone suggested that he and Minagawa went back a ways.

"You're a director too," Minagawa said to him.

"Nagai's a director?" Senda said with surprise.

"It's Club Love Incorporated now," Nagai said with disgust. "Mama's husband is president. Her little brother is a managing director." This news made Senda chuckle.

"Chen, in the kitchen, is the 'director of procurement.' The whole thing's a joke."

"Pretty soon it'll be the same story everywhere," Minagawa said smugly.

"So that makes Mama chairman?" Senda asked.

Nagai laughed loudly. "Exactly. She's got her old man on a short leash."

"By the way, would you like to have a drink somewhere else?" Senda asked.

"What—you're ready for more?" Nagai was amazed. "Look, Sen-chan, can you take care of Minagawa-san for me? I've got to get back and close up." He raised a hand in a gesture of supplication.

"Happy to," Senda said without missing a beat.

"Thanks. Well, I'll be going . . ." Nagai started to rise.

"Leaving already?" Minagawa asked.

"What do you mean 'already'? The manager has to be there before last order is called, otherwise I'll get the boot."

"I know a place you might like," Senda said to Minagawa.

"Well, now *that's* unusual," said one of the hostesses flirtatiously. "Where are you going, boss?"

"You girls stay here and keep selling."

"Selling what?" The women laughed.

"Don't pay for the drinks yourself."

"What's going on? The boss is in a good mood tonight."

Senda signaled the bartenders and left with Minagawa. "Where are we headed?" he asked.

"A bar called Tsunaki."

"Do they have nice girls?"

"They might. I haven't been there since they opened." It was close to eleven. The streets of Kabukichō were buzzing.

When they arrived at Tsunaki, Kuniko happily took them under her wing. Minagawa seemed to like the place. He sat with an arm around the Mama's shoulders and ordered drink after drink.

"I'd like to see you again, someplace else," Kuniko said in a low voice, putting a hand lightly on Senda's thigh. He was a customer, and he was with a guest. The situation had its limitations.

"When you're off tonight, come to my place."
"Yotsuya . . .?"
"Lui. Where else?"
Kuniko blushed. "I know."
Senda smiled. Things were moving right along.
After a polite interval, he left Minagawa to his drinking, walked back to Lui, sent the bartenders home early, and started tidying up while he waited for Kuniko.

He was nervous. It was just the time of night when a regular customer would show up for a nightcap. He had to keep the sign lit; if he turned it off, Kuniko might think he'd gone home.

"What, are you closing?" Sure enough, in walked one of his old customers.

"Yep, calling it a night."

"You forgot to turn off the sign." The man's name was Machino. He was an obstetrician.

"I was just about to do that," Senda said. There was nothing to do but turn the sign off.

"Feeling all right? You look down."

"No, everything's fine."

"Maybe I should examine you. Might be one of those female complaints. Whisky, neat." Machino settled his portly body on a bar stool. "I haven't sat across a bar from you in ages."

"Not since Foxx, I think." Foxx was a bar where Senda had worked years before.

"Has it been that long?"

"Sorry to keep you waiting." It was Kuniko.

Machino looked her up and down and tossed off his whisky. "Well, I'm off," he said, standing up.

"Already? Why not take your time?"

"Next time just tell me," Machino said and gave Kuniko a chivalrous smile. "What a lovely lady."

"Thank you." She smiled coquettishly.

"Senda's a good man."

"He certainly is."

"Come on, Machino," Senda said. "I think you've got the wrong idea."

"I don't make mistakes when it comes to this kind of thing. How long do you think I've been practicing?"

"Oh, you're a doctor?" Kuniko said.

"Yes. At your service." Machino went to the door. "Good night."

"One more drink," Senda said.

"You've got yourself a woman. If people hear I got in the way, I'll catch it from everyone—Pot Still and Pelican and Club Love and Golden Bear. So long." He strolled out.

"Is that how we look?" Kuniko said with a meaningful glance as Senda came out from behind the bar.

"Maybe we're a good match," Senda chuckled, slightly uncomfortable. "Well? Where shall we go?"

He took a flashy summer jacket off the hanger and turned to find Kuniko inches away. Their eyes tugged at each other.

"Wait . . ." she whispered.

"Hmm?"

"I've just met you."

"And . . .?"

"I'm not usually like this." She closed the gap between them. Senda took her into his arms as though they were already lovers. They kissed, a light kiss that went on forever.

"Come with me to Roppongi," he said and slipped into his jacket.

THE NEXT DAY IT rained. Kuniko stayed until past eleven again, this time in Senda's bed.

"I'd like to give you something to remember me." He was staring at the ceiling.

Kuniko lay half across him, her cheek against his chest. She shook her long, sleep-tousled hair.

"I don't want anything."

"Why?"

"You make it sound like it's over." They still smelled faintly of liquor.

"That's not what I meant." He stroked her hair.

"I don't want it to be over."

"I don't either."

Senda hadn't been with a woman for quite some time. Kuniko had writhed in ecstasy beneath him until dawn. It was true—there was no need to worry about their voices being heard next door. The memory of her sweet keening came back to him as he said, "Let me buy you a gift."

She snorted skeptically and kissed his chest. "If you like."

"Let's go."

He rose. Kuniko tumbled off him and lay face up. Last night, completely drained, her pale, lissome body had been like a puppet with its strings cut. Even now Senda couldn't get the image out of his mind.

"No. Let's stay in bed." She looked at him reproachfully.

"We'll never get up. Look, can you meet me tonight?"

"We'll get up in a while. Are you going to leave me like this?" She drew her knees up and let them fall open.

"Well, I guess it can't be helped." He shrugged and placed his palms together.

"Come here." She grasped his wrists and pulled him toward her. As moved into her, Senda wondered how many times they'd made love since last night.

It was past noon when they arrived in Ginza. Senda took Kuniko into the first jewelry store they saw.

"Not too expensive, now," he said for the salesman to hear as they studied the display case. "How about that one?" He put a finger on the glass. He wanted it to be a diamond.

His problem was that impression of a ring on her left hand. Even now it looked sharp and clear.

Days before, someone else's ring had been on that finger. For some reason it had disappeared, and Senda had a feeling its absence had something to do with why he and Kuniko were together. He wanted to claim that space for himself as soon as possible.

"That one."

Kuniko took a long time to show an interest in any one ring. When she did, it was a simple band with a single large stone, yet less expensive than the many others Senda tried to interest her in. He nodded and kept suggesting alternatives, but she insisted.

"It seems a bit cheap for the size of the stone," Senda said to the salesman, hoping to turn Kuniko's interest elsewhere.

"The price depends on the grade. But with stones like this one, you really get your money's worth." Contrary to Senda's strategy, the salesman started explaining why the ring was a good buy.

"Shall we get it, then?" Senda said to her finally. There was no need to adjust the size.

"I want your name on it," she whispered.

Senda told the salesman what needed to be done. "It will be ready in less than an hour," he said. They left the shop to kill time until the ring was ready.

From that day on, Senda's ring glittered on Kuniko's finger. It wasn't an engagement ring, but it was a diamond, and rumors spread quickly.

"Sen-chan, are you really getting married?" Mama, from The Pelican, sounded excited on the phone.

"Nothing's decided."

"They say it's Kuni-chan at Tsunaki."

"Mm-hm."

"We celebrated your opening and your housewarming. Your wedding will be next. You just keep them coming. What are you going to do for me?"

"Celebrate your longevity."

"Don't forget to make an offering at my funeral," she said, laughing.

The women running The Two of Us, over on the west side of the station, kept at him about the wedding schedule. "You need to set the date. You're putting us out."

"How am I doing that?"

"We have to decide what to wear. Please, not in the middle of summer."

In his typical odd fashion, Nagai went to a fortune teller for a reading on the name Kuniko Senda. "It's a great name. From middle age on, things will be even better for her. The fortune teller says you'll have two kids, give or take."

"Two children? I'm not sure about that fortune teller."

"Why?"

"Everyone has two these days. Not much risk in that prediction."

"Don't say that, you're gonna jinx things. She's your fiancé. Be a nice guy."

Everyone had decided Kuniko was wearing an engagement ring. Senda himself had a persistent feeling that rumors of his wedding would become more than rumors. Kuniko seemed head over heels whenever they met, as though she couldn't imagine life without him.

Whenever they did meet, it was raining. They started referring to their time together as "rain dates." It was silly but felt romantic. Senda's heart was leaning toward commitment with each passing day. A happy sense of anticipation was growing in him.

One day he had a visit at the condo from two strangers.

"Mr. Senda? You run a bar called Lui in Kabukichō. Correct?" One of the plainclothes cops showed him his badge.

"Yes, that's me. Is there a problem?"

"Nothing major. We hear you bought a ring recently."

Senda started laughing. "Oh, no . . ."

"No?"

"I mean . . ." Senda waved a hand in apology. "All my friends are after me about that ring."

"Why would that be?"

"They think I'm engaged or something. It's not true. I haven't decided anything."

"We're not here to investigate your marriage plans."

"I'm sure you're not, being the police and all. Not private detectives." Senda chuckled again.

"Where did you buy that ring?"

"Ginza. Tōkō Jewelry. Did something happen there?"

"No. Just wanted to know," the man said evasively. Senda was used to the way law enforcement types responded when the questions were turned on them.

"Guess he's on the up-and-up," the other detective said. They went away looking faintly disappointed.

Kuniko spent every third night with Senda. His condo started to acquire signs of feminine presence—floral-patterned undergarments, negligées, pajamas . . .

"Are you putting on weight, Sen-chan?"

Senda had stopped by Zelkova Bar for a drink. The Master, who was nicknamed Ue-chan, was studying him carefully.

"Am I?"

"Maybe because fall is coming?"

"And I'm getting fat like a horse? Is what you mean?"

"Not exactly. But it's strange." The Master grinned. "You ought to be thinner after all that time with Kuniko."

"All right. I was wondering when we were going to get to that."

"I'm not joking. It really is strange. When a young woman has a man in her life, her jaw line starts to fill out. But it's happening to you too."

"Okay, that's enough. I get it. I should just get married, right?"

"You're going to do it?" The Master's eyes opened wide.

"Yeah, for you. Because you won't leave me alone."

"I knew it!" the Master shouted. He threw himself at the phone on the wall and started dialing frantically.

"Pelican? Is Mama there? It's Ue. I'm here with Sen-chan. Listen, he says he's gonna do it. He just told me. Here, just now."

He pressed the hook, lifted it, and started dialing again.

"I'm out of here," Senda said.

"Fine. Go home. Get back there and get married. Hello? Zelkova. Sen-chan's going to do it!"

"Oh, hell." Senda couldn't laugh it off any more. It was hopeless. He got up and walked out.

"It rains, and I end up getting married," he muttered to himself as he walked back to Lui.

It went on raining almost every day. The rumor got around that it always rained when Senda and Kuniko were together. He started getting calls whenever the skies opened.

"Hey, it's Nagai."

"What?"

"Is she there?"

"Uh-huh."

"Ah. All right, then. Nothing special."

Senda hung up. "Who was that?" a sleepy Kuniko called from the bed.

"Open the curtains."

"Why? Oh, it's raining again."

"Now you know." Senda went back to the bed. The phone rang.

"Aren't you going to answer?"

"Leave it. It's another idiot checking on us."

"You don't have to get mad about it." She turned away and went back to sleep.

Those were days of honey, and they lasted until December. But with the new year, Kuniko started pulling away little by little. Senda didn't wake up to what was happening until spring was just around the corner.

"Good morning."

"Well, this is unusual." Senda stepped aside to let Mama from The Pelican come in. She peered around the room, even peeked into the bedroom.

"I knew it. Something's wrong."

"What are you talking about?"

"I've got bad news for you. You better prepare yourself."

"That sounds scary." Senda went into the kitchen and started preparing tea. "It's about Kuniko, I guess," he called.

"Oh dear, you've heard?"

"No, but things are going a bit sideways."

Senda put two cups of Earl Grey on the table and sat facing Mama.

"She has a boyfriend."

"Really? I haven't noticed a thing. But it makes sense."

"He's with the mob. And he's a gigolo. The police have him now. He's a bottom feeder. A petty fence."

"The mob . . ."

"Better steer clear."

Senda couldn't believe that a woman like Kuniko would get mixed up with criminals.

"The thing is, it looks like he used to live right around the corner from you."

"Around the corner . . .?" Senda thought back to their first meeting.

"I heard it from a cop I know at the Yotsuya Police Station. He told me to tell you, watch out."

"You mean Kurosawa?"

"That's the one. Oh, this tea is delicious." She took another sip. "A jewelry store was robbed. A team of four, I think. The police think Kuniko might be involved."

"You're joking."

"This guy, her boyfriend or whatever, is a known fence. Kuniko likes precious stones. The police thought she was wearing one of the stolen diamonds. But they got that wrong. I mean, it's your ring, isn't it?"

The world was dimming before Senda's eyes. For a moment all he could see was the mark of someone else's ring on that pale, slender finger.

"Sen-chan? This isn't like you. Get a grip." Mama was staring at him. "It happens all the time," she continued. "Look, why don't you come by my place tonight? Everyone will be there. They're up for a little gambling party. We haven't had one for ages."

"Gambling," Senda repeated absently.

"Sure. Cards, mahjong, whatever you like."

"I'll be there."

"Don't change your mind. Lots of people will be disappointed if you do. I've got loose lips, I'll admit it. They're not coming just to gamble." She stood up. "You know what I mean, don't you?"

Senda went to Mama's house that night and partied

until dawn. When he got back to the condo, he knew that Kuniko had spent the night.

The connection between a woman and a man is hard to sever. All through that spring, Senda often wore a dark look. Even after her secret had been exposed, Kuniko had clung to him, apologizing, weeping, panicking again and again. But toward the end of May she disappeared. Her gigolo had gotten out of jail.

Senda's ring had helped prove her innocence. Later he heard that her man had been arrested the morning they met. She would've ditched the stolen ring just before the downpour. Its place had been taken by Senda's gift, which was close to identical. That was why Kuniko had insisted on that particular ring.

The early summer rain fell every day, and every day Senda thought of her with sadness. Everything had started with that sudden downpour.

It came to him one day as he stood at the window, looking out at another shower. "She needed me for shelter from the rain. But it never rains forever," he murmured.

Somehow it made sense.

Back to the Old Days

Kyōko and Yoshie were killing time on the furniture floor of Isetan Department Store when they ran straight into Satoko, the Mama of The Golden Bear.

The Golden Bear was a large hostess bar—a "cabaret"—in Kabukichō, not far from Seibu Shinjuku Station. Satoko was a fixture in the neighborhood; she'd put down roots there soon after the war.

When the two women saw the corpulent Mama, they hurriedly put on formal expressions and bowed respectfully.

"Doing some shopping?" Satoko asked. Her welcoming smile put Kyōko and Yoshie off balance. Not knowing what to say, they answered vaguely.

"Who's getting married? Don't tell me it's both of you," Satoko laughed. They were standing in a section of vanities with triple mirrors, surrounded by reflections of themselves.

At first the young women didn't grasp what she was getting at. After a moment of confusion, Kyōko said brightly, "Oh my, no. That's not it at all. We're just out for a stroll. Right?" She looked at Yoshie.

"Yes, that's it," Yoshie said with a grave expression.

"Oh, that's too bad. Running into you here made me feel sure something auspicious must be coming."

"And you? Are you shopping today?" Kyōko asked, a bit stiffly.

"Yes. The daughter of a friend of mine is getting married. Anyway, I'm finished. Would you like to have coffee?"

"We'd love to!" the ladies said in unison. Satoko was, without a doubt, a prominent elder. She seemingly had personal connections with every circle of Mamas and Masters in the Shinjuku bar business; Kyōko and Yoshie 'belonged' to one of these circles, but they had learned the business from people who'd learned from people mentored by Satoko. She'd never spoken to them one-on-one, and when their circle got together, they only saw her from across the room. As they followed her to the escalator, they stared at each other, nonplussed.

"I envy you two," the Mama said, turning to look up at them as they descended. "It's so wonderful to be young." After years in the business, her heavy makeup had left her face deeply lined. Looking down at her, the women could see plainly that she colored her hair.

"Your clothes suit you wonderfully," Kyōko ventured. She thought she had to fill the moment with something.

"Don't be absurd," Satoko said with a dry laugh as she glanced at Kyōko with reproachful eyes.

Kyōko turned to Yoshie. "This is the first time I've seen her in Western clothes," she said earnestly, trying to smother the rebuke she'd just been handed.

"I wish I could wear jeans like you girls. They would've been perfect back in the black market days."

The young women laughed to cover their bafflement. For Satoko, the sprawling warren of stalls outside Shinjuku Station remained a vivid memory; it had been the only way to obtain so much that was essential to a semblance of normal life in the first years after the defeat. But to Yoshie and Kyōko, she might as well have been talking about topknots and rickshaws.

They stopped at a coffee shop in the basement of Isetan. After fifteen minutes of chatting about this and that, they went their separate ways.

"See? She knew exactly who we were," Kyōko said.

"We better learn from her," Yoshie nodded. They were giddy that someone as exalted as Satoko deigned to recognize them. It was like being "friends" with a celebrity.

It was time to get The Two of Us, their little counter bar, ready for the evening, so they headed toward the west side of the station. One other person worked there, a young man who doubled as bar manager and bartender. Because they were partners, Yoshie and Kyōko were both Mamas.

As they walked through the tunnel that passed under the elevated line, linking the east side of the station to the west side, they ran into another elder of the bar scene.

"Hi there . . ." called a man with streaks of gray in his hair as he ambled slowly toward them.

"Hello, Nagai-san."

"What are you guys doing dressed like guys? You're wasting your assets."

Nagai was the manager of Club Love, a bar on Kaname Street. The three of them started chatting in the middle of the narrow passage. Kyōko grinned. "I saw you, you know."

"Doing what?"

"Last Sunday. You and your wife, outside Keio Department Store."

"Oh, that."

"I'm gonna tell Kozue, over at Salomé."

"Don't scare me like that, you idiot!"

"It's not a threat. I'll tell her for real."

"Don't even joke about it. Look, I was taking my wife to Fuchū, that's all."

"To the race track?"

"Yeah, there's a bus from right out front of Keio. That's all it was. Nothing romantic or anything. It's not like I was having fun."

Kozue was Nagai's Achilles heel. She was a young hostess he'd helped open her own bar, naturally behind his wife's back. The wife was known to be crazy about the horses, and Kozue was notorious for her jealousy.

"In that case I'll let it pass," Kyōko said. She and Yoshie looked at each other and laughed.

"Where've you guys been today?" Nagai's question made them both stand up straighter.

"Satoko treated us," Yoshie said.

"Satoko . . .?" Nagai was astonished. "What for?"

"She told us we're the future of Shinjuku."

"She said that?"

Both women shrugged. Nagai studied them through narrowed eyes and clicked his tongue. "That's not good. No, that's not good," he murmured half to himself. "Well, see you," he added and walked quickly away.

"Weird as usual." Yoshie laughed.

"He's got the wrong idea about something again," Kyōko said as she watched Nagai's retreating back. As he walked toward the late afternoon sunlight at the end of the tunnel, he became a black silhouette.

After he left the girls, Nagai made his way across Yasukuni Avenue into Kabukichō and down the stairs to Lui.

"Good morning. . . ."

"Nagai-san." Ishii, one of the bartenders, waved from a corner of the dimly lit room.

"Is that you, Ishii? Turn the sign on," Nagai said in wheedling tone. "Look like you're doing business."

"Sorry, just opened."

"Is Senda in yet?"

"He was here. He should be over at Cactus."

"Cactus..." Now he was even more worried. He sprinted up the stairs to the street.

Cactus was a coffee shop on the first two floors of a building across the street. Since Senda had opened Lui, Cactus had become an early evening hangout for his circle from the neighborhood. Nagai put his face to the big bay window and peered inside. Senda saw him and waved.

"Oh, you've got company," Nagai said as he approached the table. Senda was with two other men. Nagai looked slightly surprised as he bowed to one of them. "Oketani-san..."

"Good timing," the man said, making room for him on the bench seat. About thirty, he was a fixture at Lui and Club Love.

"Coffee for me," Nagai called to the waitress.

"Oke-chan heard something strange today," Senda said.

"Really? Always has his ear to the ground. So what's up?"

"Ibaragi Tamayoshi." The second man, whose name was Murokawa, spoke in a quiet, conspiratorial tone. He ran a jazz coffee shop near Isetan.

"I've heard of him." Nagai nodded. "From Osaka. Big bucks."

"That's him. Ibaragi Corporation opened a branch in Ginza seven or eight years back and started a chain of high-end cabarets. Very aggressive." Oketani's day job was broking real estate in Ginza. He was an expert when it came to bars and nightlife properties.

"Ibaragi seems to be tied to the mob," Murokawa said.

"No kidding," Nagai said. "He's expanding into Shinjuku."

"What, you know already?" The two men looked crestfallen.

"And he's going after Golden Bear," Nagai added.

"That's right. There's that Chinese place next door. And the Korean barbecue."

"Those two and Golden Bear are the oldest buildings in the neighborhood," Nagai said. "Ibaragi probably bought the eateries already. If he can get Satoko to sell, he'd have enough of a footprint for a good-size building. He's putting a lot of pressure on her. Even I know that much."

"Well, you're right, and that's why we're worried. Satoko is a fighter. That's her strong point, but she's no match for someone like Ibaragi."

"Listen, that's the reason I got myself over here as fast as I could."

"What happened?" Nagai's audience leaned forward expectantly.

"I think Satoko might be cracking. She's getting old. The thing is, she treated a couple of our young ladies to a nice meal."

"Young ladies?"

"Yeah. She told them they were the future of Shinjuku. To me that smells like she's retiring."

Oketani and Murokawa looked grave.

"So it's true. We're losing The Golden Bear . . ."

"Who were these two ladies, anyway?" Senda asked.

"The Two of Us ladies."

Senda laughed wryly. "Those guys? I don't believe it."

"Well, you better," Nagai said. "I just ran into them. They told me all about it."

"Kyōko and Yoshie? The future of Shinjuku? Something's wrong with that picture."

"Why? Don't you believe me? Now that I think about it, they're very reliable. All they need is some seasoning, and the future of Shinjuku . . ."—he lost momentum suddenly—" . . . might be okay."

Senda laughed. "Are you sure Satoko treated them to a meal?"

"That's what they said. Then they went off, both of them in jeans."

"Nagai-san, that's impossible." Murokawa looked at him piercingly. "So you're saying Satoko invites them to lunch—if it's you or me, okay, that would be different—but she invites them, and they show up in jeans? Come on."

Nagai stared blankly at him, mouth half-open. When his coffee arrived, he busied himself adding sugar and stirring with a vengeance. "What kind of beans do they use here? Mocha? Maybe Brazilian . . ."

Murokawa persisted. "Are you sure they weren't pulling your leg?"

"Whatever they're using, it's great coffee."

"I give up," Murokawa said and smiled at Oketani.

"Anyway," Nagai said, holding his cup, "I'm worried. You know about what." His audience nodded. "We've got to do something."

"We were just talking about it," Murokawa said. "Satoko's pretty strong-willed. If we offer help the wrong way, she'll box our ears."

"True. Everyone who could stand up to her for more than five minutes is dead or gone when she needs them most. I bet she feels alone right now."

"You're the only one who can talk to her, Nagai."

"I guess. But if the conversation goes sideways, she'll get out of hand."

"Let's find out as much as we can. This is happening on our territory, in Shinjuku. If we work together we ought to be able to ferret out the details."

"The Golden Bear . . ." Nagai stared at some invisible horizon. He was looking back to a time when he and everyone around him was young, when life seemed to be a road that only led upward.

Satoko had been one of the most successful people in their circle. Her cabaret was an aging wooden building now, but when it opened soon after the war, it had been a top-drawer establishment. For old Shinjuku hands, it was a shining symbol of their youth—even now, when it was dwarfed by the buildings around it.

That was how The Golden Bear Preservation Association, as they might have christened it, was launched in Cactus Coffee Shop.

Later that evening, Senda phoned The Two of Us, on the far side of the station.

"Hello? Two of Us." Senda heard the familiar voice on the line.

"It's Senda, Kyōko."

"Oh, nice to hear from you."

"You said something to Nagai-san today?"

"We saw him on the street this afternoon. What's this about?"

"Is it true Satoko treated you and Yoshie?"

"That's right."

"Where did she take you?"

"For coffee."

Senda clicked his tongue in disgust. "So that's all it was."

"We ran into her in Isetan. We were amazed she even remembered who we are."

"Did she say anything in particular to you?"

"Not really. I get it—Nagai-san's having another one of his fantasies."

"Never mind. Listen, if you hear about anything going on with The Golden Bear, let me know, will you?"

"Is something going on?"

"I'll fill you in next time. Keep your ears open."

Senda hung up and started dialing another friend.

For two months nothing happened, but Ibaragi's money was clearly making waves in Shinjuku. The Korean barbecue and the Chinese restaurant next to Satoko's cabaret passed into his hands.

He must've been putting pressure on Satoko as well, but no one could get anything out of her. They were worried about losing a symbol of their youth, but Nagai and the others were having a hard time finding out anything. Satoko was too proud to ask for help; the Golden Bear had done a lot to get Kabukichō off the ground just after the war.

"I'm not worried," Nagai told his confederates whenever they gathered. "Satoko's not the kind of woman to let a few threats drive her out."

His listeners were ready to agree. Only Senda and the Mama of The Pelican saw it differently.

"You call Ibaragi an outsider," Mama said to Nagai, "but Shinjuku is full of outsiders. And even if all of us were Shinjuku natives, times have changed. People with this"—she made a circle with thumb and forefinger and thrust it in Nagai's face—"always win. I don't know how much Satoko has saved up, but I'm sure she doesn't have enough to fight off someone like Ibaragi."

"Since when have you been so money-mad?"

"I'm not. That's the point. You should know better than anyone. The Golden Bear is part of us. We all want money, but we're not like Ibaragi. We do things differently. If we didn't, we'd all be richer. The Golden Bear represents all of us. Walk over to Seibu Shinjuku. Take a look around. There are still lots of little buildings, wooden buildings, between the office towers. That makes people like us happy, but when the money comes in, they'll tear it all down. It should've happened by now."

One evening, Senda was behind the bar when he got an urgent call from The Pelican.

"Drop everything and get over here right away. It's urgent."

"Lui's packed."

"Who cares? Your bar's not important."

"Mama, get serious."

"I am serious. Satoko's in trouble."

"I'll be right there."

Senda dashed out the door toward The Pelican. When he got there, Mama said cuttingly, "You missed him. See? He's gone."

"Who?"

"I'll tell you. Just sit down." She practically dragged him to an open seat near the entrance. "Just a few minutes ago, the branch manager at Mitsubishi was sitting right there."

"Konno-san?"

"That's right. He told me Satoko asked for a loan. She's been dealing with him for years and years."

"A loan for what?"

"Construction. He said Satoko wants to put up a new building."

Senda was silent as he took this in. Finally he said, "She wants Ibaragi off her back."

"Exactly. The thing is, the bank rejected the request."

"Her credit's no good?"

Mama shook her head. "Konno-san was leaning toward lending her the money, but his boss said no. He was just on his way back from breaking the news to her when he stopped by to whisper in my ear. He says it looks like Ibaragi pressured headquarters to deny the loan."

"I'm impressed. He must have a lot of pull."

"Stop praising him, you idiot. Ibaragi wants to take Satoko down. What are we going to do?"

"What are you asking me for?"

"You're no help at all! Come on, get a grip. There must be an angle we can play here, some kind of angle."

"Bankers... I've got a few banker customers, but they're not very high up the ladder."

"What about Moriyama at Sumitomo? Or Ogawa at Daiichi?"

"Not good enough."

"Look, you have to do something. If the bank angle's no good, then construction companies. Someone who'll put up Satoko's building on credit."

"A whole building on credit?" Senda looked at Mama with astonishment. He and his circle of friends didn't cater to the heavy hitters. As an opponent, Ibaragi Corporation was just too powerful.

Next morning Senda was woken by a ringing phone.

"Sen-chan..."

"All right, who is this?"

"Rumiko. From Kent."

"Do you know what time it is?"

"It's awful, Sen-chan. I was on the way home this morning, heading for Seibu Shinjuku. I saw a bunch of trucks. They're getting ready to demolish The Golden Bear."

"Say that again?" Senda was suddenly wide awake. "Are you sure?"

"Yes. They're tearing down the buildings next door, too."

"Shit!"

"What can we do? Senda, what can we do?" Rumiko was in tears.

"We'll get everyone together. Let's see—come to my place. Give me half an hour, forty minutes."

He hung up and called Nagai, Mama, and Murokawa, then bolted out the door.

Rumiko arrived moments after he opened up the bar. "This morning's the first time I was glad I cheated," she said, hunching her shoulders against the cold. "If I hadn't been walking by just then, I wouldn't've known they were tearing down The Golden Bear."

"Everyone should be here soon. Watch the place for me, will you?"

"Where are you going?"

"To check it out."

Senda hurried toward Seibu Shinjuku Station. When he arrived, he saw a crew of workers pulling down both restaurants, just as Rumiko had said. By now the buildings were a heap of ruins. But when he looked closer, he saw The Golden Bear was untouched.

He returned to Lui feeling deflated. "Thanks a lot," he scolded Rumiko. "You had me going there."

"But everyone says Golden Bear's in danger. When I saw what was happening, I assumed the worst." She grimaced. "See? I shouldn't have cheated after all," she added, crestfallen.

Nagai hurried in with hair looking like a haystack, followed by a neatly dressed Murokawa. His jazz coffee shop closed at eight in the morning.

"It's still there. What a relief," Nagai said.

"But they're up to something for sure," Murokawa insisted.

Mama arrived a few minutes later. "I was planning to let everyone know this afternoon. It looks like Ibaragi is opening his own place where those restaurants were."

"What kind of place?" everyone said at once.

"A cabaret. He's going to steal Satoko's business."

"Are you sure?" Nagai said.

"Oke-chan was in last night and told me. Some guy named Oikawa is managing the project for Ibaragi. Somehow or other they're going to force Satoko to sell."

"Makes sense," Murokawa said. "Damage her business to beat the price down."

"Ibaragi has lots of bars in Osaka. He'll be bringing hostesses from there for the new place. According to Oke-chan, it'll be like they're on a business trip. Ibaragi will put them up at some hotel for as long as it takes."

"And lean on Satoko until she cracks."

"Oke-chan said they're bringing the prettiest girls. The whole thing's unbelievable."

At this, Nagai burst out laughing. "What's gotten into you?" Mama said.

"What do you think? This Ibaragi is a fool."

"How so?"

"Look. I don't know whose dumb idea this was, but he doesn't know what he's doing. Of all the strategies they could've used, I mean, going head-to-head with a cabaret?"

"He's right." Mama struck her palm. "That's it. They think they'll be competing with one cabaret, Golden Bear. We won't let them. The Golden Bear is each and every one of us. Satoko's place is just the headquarters." She clapped Nagai on the shoulder, and they laughed heartily.

"This'll be interesting. Let them build their cabaret," he said.

"Yes, let them try it. We're with Satoko."

Senda and Murokawa exchanged glances. Murokawa had a hot temper; he was grinning wolfishly at the thought of a fight.

"Sen-chan, this is going to be fun. It doesn't matter how many girls they send from Osaka. They're not going to beat us on our own ground. We'll use every trick in the book to run them out of here."

Senda ducked behind the counter and got the kettle going. "I should be serving drinks, but it's morning, so let's go with Earl Grey."

"With a shot of whisky." Mama laughed.

"She's right. They can send the best gunslingers in Osaka, but we're still faster on the draw." Nagai was a fan of Westerns.

"They'll probably put on a beauty pageant. Send some hostesses over from Ginza, too."

"Good. That'll play right into our hands. Everybody tries to corner the market on beauty, but it never works. We'll send the cream of the crop over to Satoko." Nagai's confidence was unshakeable. "I'll put together a roster. We'll get the best talent."

Rumiko wasn't so sure. "What if they bring musicians and show people to perform?"

"Fine. Let them."

"But they can get celebrities."

"Don't worry," Senda cut in. "They'll get more people in, but it'll cost them. Name talent will pull people from outside Shinjuku. As soon as the talent are gone, those customers disappear. They can use top-end hostesses and stars to pack them in, but it won't pay. The Golden Bear has a different clientele."

"He's right. Listen, Rumiko," Murokawa said. "The biggest threat is that Ibaragi will come in with an authentic Osaka cabaret setup. If he does, we'll have a problem. But he's already operating in Ginza, with a pure Ginza strategy. Maybe it works there, but it won't work here."

Murokawa whispered something in Mama's ear. "Oh—*that's* a good idea," she said.

"What?" Nagai said, curious. "Come on."

"Well . . ." Mama glanced at Murokawa again before saying brightly, "Until this war is over, let's have Misawa give us some leeway."

"Misawa? You mean the foot patrol?"

"Why not? He goes way back. We've had lots of run-ins with him and his men over the years, but he wouldn't want to see Satoko chased out of business."

"That's brilliant." Nagai couldn't suppress his excitement. He stood up. "We can use our secret weapon."

"As in . . .?" Rumiko said.

"Full contact, no panties."

"Just until we run Ibaragi out," Mama added.

"I wonder if girls from those sorts of bars would be willing to help out," Rumiko said.

"They just might." Nagai's blood was up.

THE NEW CABARET OPENED. Rows of floral wreaths adorned with "Ibaragi Corporation" banners were arrayed outside. The same day, Satoko's allies gathered at The Golden Bear.

"Let us do this," Nagai pleaded. "Giving up without a fight is no way to go."

"Of course this is hard on me," Satoko said. "But I can't lean on other people for help."

"Sakura-san, you're wrong." Nagai sounded almost threatening. "If you do nothing, you're sure to lose. And you're not leaning on 'other people' for help. I'm telling you, let us do this. This is us, okay? You remember what things were like around here, way back. This whole area around Seibu Shinjuku."

Satoko gazed at Nagai and the rest of the room. "I remember."

"There was one road, surfaced with crushed slag. Rows of little shops on both sides, in Quonset huts. Somebody put up a cheap arch at the end of the road. They spread the slag thick, so the road would last. It came up to the doorsteps of the huts."

Kyōko and Senda were sitting at the back of the group. "What's 'slag'?" she asked Senda in a low voice.

"What you get when you burn coke."

"Oh, that."

When the elders were together, talking about those

distant days, younger people like Senda and Kyōko sat at the back and made themselves small. There were faces at the front of the crowd that Senda didn't recognize. Some would've been people in the business who moved out of Shinjuku long ago or people who'd gotten out of the business or even some who'd never been in the business at all. But they all remembered those departed days when The Golden Bear first flourished.

Also in front was a well-known cop, though he was out of uniform. "Madam, why don't you let these people show what they can do for you?"

"Officer Misawa—you too?" Satoko rolled her eyes.

"I know how you feel. Of all the people here today, you're the one with the least attachment to this place."

"What's that mean?" Nagai took a step toward him.

"Not what you think."

"Then what?"

"Times have changed. You're all in the business because you love people. If you can spend every evening with your customers, you're satisfied. And you make a decent living at it. There's no business better. Anyway that's what I think.

"But things are changing fast. For better or worse, no one can say. Obviously things are going to change. Madam knows that as well as anyone. Say 'Madam' in Shinjuku and everyone thinks of The Golden Bear. It didn't used to be that way. You had to ask 'Which Madam?' Today everyone is 'Mama.' 'Madam' sounds old-fashioned.

"Things change. You've done everything you set out to do. Now you're thinking, if it's going to end because times have changed, let it end. Even if Ibaragi hadn't shown up, establishments that are out of step with the times will disappear. That's how you see it."

"You're right. Listen to me, all of you." Satoko sat up straight, leaned forward, and peered at everyone in the room. "I could keep The Golden Bear operating in Shinjuku for a long time, easily. I could redo the inside to keep up with the times. But I haven't. I know what I 'should' do. This is my place, after all."

"Why didn't you?" someone said.

"I didn't want to. I wanted to drop dead from a stroke or a heart attack while my customers were still enjoying this place the way it is. But I was too strong."

"You'll live to be a hundred, Madam," someone else shouted, but no one laughed.

"I'm glad I left The Golden Bear just as it is. Especially now. Do you know why?"

No one spoke. All eyes were on her.

"Whenever there's an emergency, everyone gathers here. Like tonight. What if I'd renovated this place? Or torn it down and put up a building? If I'd changed with the times, I would've lost touch with all of you. But to be honest, I wouldn't've cared." She bit her lower lip.

"I'm like the rest of you. I don't want Shinjuku to change. That's who I am. I want things to be like they were in the old days, when people were satisfied with cheap drinks and cheap food. You're here because you feel the way I do. Ibaragi's no big threat. He's just something else that's happening to The Golden Bear. I can't do a thing to control it. So I've decided not to waste time fighting it."

"There you have it," Misawa said. "The Golden Bear is fading into the sunset. Let it go in peace."

"Can it, you stupid cop!" Murokawa stepped forward, rolling up his coat sleeve. "Come on, Misawa. You've been chasing us for years. I thought you knew the score, but I was wrong."

"About what?" The cop flushed with anger.

"Fading into the sunset? Give up before we're beaten? Yeah, I understand what Madam said. We're all behind the times. We'd rather burn our businesses to the ground than chase trends and operate without a soul.

"That's why we all have small places, even now. We could've made them bigger. We know what to do. We just won't. That's the way we are. But how can we hand The Golden Bear over to someone who doesn't care about our town? The new Shinjuku can take care of itself. We can all disappear, okay? And we will, someday. But we want to pass on at least a bit of our way of doing things to the people who come after us, even Ibaragi. Right? We want to put a scare into him. We want him to understand what Shinjuku is, that's all. That's why we're doing this."

"He's right," Nagai said. "Even after things change, don't we want people to remember what kind of town this used to be?"

"I know how you feel, but . . ." Misawa started to answer, but Satoko broke in.

"Why don't we do it, then?" she said with a mischievous smile. The crowd murmured its approval.

"Give the word, Madam!" a woman called.

"Officer—we don't have a plan yet, but while we're going up against Ibaragi, give us a little leeway, okay?"

"As long as it's not violent, I'll let it slide. I don't like Ibaragi either." Misawa grinned.

"Then it's decided," Nagai said, looking relieved. "In fact, I've already borrowed four or five terrific ladies from a cabaret in Uguisudani. Amazing. They'll let you do anything." People parted to make way for him as he hurried out.

"Madam, please let us help too," Kyōko said shyly.

"What about your bar?"

"It's all right. We asked our regulars to bring their business here."

Satoko smiled in wonderment. "Really? You've got some good customers."

"We'll ask other customers with nothing going on to come too."

Satoko laughed. "You're amazing. Customers with nothing going on? Even I wasn't that cheeky when I was young."

No one knew where he'd stashed them, but Nagai soon returned, trailing five young women. They seemed a bit put out.

IBARAGI'S CABARET WAS CALLED Goldfinger. The building was festooned with neon. Every night there was a show with celebrity vocalists. The new establishment was clearly attracting more customers than The Golden Bear, but most of them were casual visitors drawn by the flashy advertisements.

The Golden Bear had never been flashy, but customers walking through the door were struck with a wave of feverish energy from the crowded room. The hostesses memorized customer preferences instantly, and for those with a taste for it, there were young ladies who were adept at more personalized forms of attention.

The almost anarchic, semi-lawless atmosphere was straight out of Shinjuku's golden age. The hors d'oeuvres were cheap and the girls were experts at measuring customers' wallets. The Golden Bear sent everyone home satisfied.

Nagai, Murokawa, and Senda served as waiters, hoisting silver trays of drinks. The royalty of Shinjuku gathered, the movers and shakers, each with his kingdom and castle.

The party was on. It was out of control. Everyone was carousing the old Shinjuku way.

"I see our massage ladies are getting the hang of things," Nagai said with a look of satisfaction as he surveyed the scene from the edge of the room.

Ue-chan from Zelkova Bar agreed. "They're having fun. This is a new twist for them. I hear table twelve went all the way last night."

"So did I. I was here, and I didn't even notice. Which girl?"

"One of the crew from Uguisudani. See? There she is. Drunk again. In twenty minutes she'll have her gear off."

"Must be a professional habit."

Most of the customers knew exactly how the old Shinjuku operated. There were examiners from the tax office, bankers, and managers from the big department stores.

Oketani knew the people at Ibaragi Corporation from his work in Ginza. He took up a discrete position near the door and would alert the waiters whenever a spy from Goldfinger arrived to check out the action. Oddly, Ibaragi's spies partied as hard as everyone else.

Nagai dispatched his best crews to service these spies. Easily taken in, they would act like big shots, pawing the "special" hostesses recruited from Ueno, Ikebukuro, and as far away as Koiwa until nearly closing time.

"Welcome to Shinjuku," Nagai would mutter with satisfaction as he watched another spy stagger out the door.

The floor shows were a shout-out from the past. They were somewhat seedy, the kind of seedy that was once a Shinjuku trademark. The shows matched the old building perfectly, and their very cheapness drove the excitement to greater heights.

"SENDA ... I DON'T WANT to go home ..." Several evenings into the campaign, Nagai was sitting with a drink in his hand and tears in his eyes. "This is like a dream. I could wander all over Japan and never find a place like this."

Senda was just as awestruck. "It'd go bust pretty quickly."

Ue-chan laughed. "You got that right. This is Satoko's swan song."

"You think so?" Nagai sighed.

"Yeah. She's repaying her customers with true cabaret culture."

"There's nothing more we could ask for."

Senda couldn't help feeling moved. Satoko wasn't just pulling out all the stops to give back to her customers. This was how she thanked her old friends in the business.

"I don't believe it. Ochiai-san!" Nagai shouted suddenly, half-crazed, and grabbed Senda's hand in his excitement. They rushed to the door.

"Ah, it's you, Nagai. Still alive and kicking. I heard Satoko brought back the old Shinjuku. I had to see for myself. Get ready—I brought a lot of people."

Nagai looked past him and saw a crowd of about thirty people in the street. "We'll make room. Senda?"

Conjuring seating out of thin air was an old Senda technique. Now he demonstrated the wizardry he used to be famous for. In a few moments, he'd rounded up enough empty chairs from a seemingly packed room to seat the whole party.

"We need more girls," Nagai said. "See to these guys while I scoop some up."

"Got it."

It was a strange night at The Golden Bear. First, Nagai got his wires crossed with his wife and girlfriend—Kozue, the Mama of Salomé Bar—and ended up calling both of them in to help out on the same day. The place was so busy that no one noticed they were both on deck until nearly closing time.

"I haven't seen Ochiai for years. I'm amazed he came tonight."

"Who was he?" Kyōko asked. "He seemed very important."

"He's a Mitsubishi big shot. I knew him when he was just starting out. He got too important and stopped coming in. I'd forgotten about him."

"He brought a huge group with him . . . Oh no! Nagai-san!"

"What?" Nagai was startled by Kyōko's sudden urgency.

"*That's* what. Look!" She pointed a trembling finger. Nagai's jaw dropped. His wife and Kozue stood glaring at each other on the other side of the room.

"Not good," Nagai croaked. The room fell silent.

"Well, Kozue, you've been a big help tonight," Nagai's wife said with daggers in her voice.

"Hold on there." Nagai was dumbfounded. "You knew?"

"Yes. She's known for a long time," Kozue said defiantly. "Are you angry, Mrs. Nagai?"

"Angry? Why? Don't misjudge me. I married that man. I worked alongside him. A woman who marries into the business has to be ready for cheating. It doesn't mean a thing to me."

"Magnificent!" Nagai shouted from the sidelines.

"That's wonderful." Kozue laughed, relieved. "To be honest, I feel the same way. When you cheat with a man in the business, you'd better be ready for him to have one or two girlfriends besides you and the wife. I promised myself I wouldn't let it upset me."

"Where am I going to find enough energy to handle more women?" Nagai said, mouth agape.

"What do you think, Sen-chan?" Murokawa said. "Ever seen anything like this?"

"Never."

"We're quite a bunch."

No one laughed. The silence was a bit cheerless. Everyone was worn out.

"Listen everybody!" Up on the stage, Satoko stuck her head out from the wings. "They're shutting Goldfinger down. It's going to be a restaurant!"

A cheer went up. Nagai started dancing a jig. Murokawa and Senda watched as everyone else rushed the stage. "They didn't put up much of a fight," Murokawa said.

"Not a very efficient use of their capital, that's for sure," Senda said wearily. "Launching a business just to intimidate someone? That's not a great strategy."

All too briefly, it had been just like the old days. Now the fun was over. It was enough to bring tears to their eyes.

Fooltown

WHEN I STUMBLED ACROSS Komai Keisuke, it was past ten on a night in early summer.

I was near Kaname Street, at the entrance to a narrow lane not far from the old vaudeville theater. I'd been spending a lot of time at one of the nearby bars. When I was out on sales calls, I could usually tie up the day's loose ends from pay phones around the station without going back to the office. For a while I didn't have a reason to be in Shinjuku, but when my territory shifted to the busiest part of town, I became a regular again more or less naturally.

I went to Waseda, so I knew Shinjuku from way back. In my student days, District Two was still a licensed quarter, and the area around Hanazono Shrine was a thriving unlicensed red-light district. The area around the shrine still has a lot of the flavor of old Shinjuku, but after coming back to the area, I was less interested in that part of town. I pretty much stuck close to Kaname Street.

I'd known Komai as a teenager. When I recognized him, time seemed to run backward, and I was in the red-light district again. It took a few seconds before I came to my senses. Komai had been a classmate in my high school on the old east side of Tokyo. I'd never been out on the piss with him or even been in Shinjuku with him.

Komai was a few yards in front of me. I'd just left my

first pub of the evening and wasn't too buzzed, but the man ahead of me was fairly drunk and unsteady on his feet. The neon sign of a massage parlor had shorted and was making a nasty sparking noise. The tout, a fixture in the neighborhood, stood under the sign calling to passers-by with a sales pitch so rapid and slurred, it was hard to make out what he was saying.

Komai seemed badly downcast, even from behind. He was walking slowly and unsteadily, and I was catching up quickly. If I'd overtaken him, the encounter would've ended with another passing in the Shinjuku night, but when I was five or six steps away, he spun around suddenly and came straight toward me.

"Huh?" He spoke first. It was clear from the look on his face that he knew me. I didn't recognize him right away, but seeing his expression, I stopped in my tracks.

"What're you doin' here?" he said in a drunken voice. I was probably smiling uncertainly. "It's me. It's Komai."

"Wait a minute..." I remembered. It was a face I hadn't seen in more than twenty years. "Komai! Why, if it isn't Komai Keisuke!"

He thrust out a hand and shook mine. His hand was moist and soft. "You got old."

"And you got fat." We kept on pumping our hands up and down.

"Out by yourself?"

When I nodded, he seemed overjoyed and invited me for a drink. I'd been planning a bar circuit anyway, so I had no objections.

"I know a place. Come on," he said excitedly. I was coming from work and had my coat and tie on. Komai was wearing a short-sleeved polo shirt. I was used to almost reflexively sizing up people's level of prosperity, but with Komai it was hard to tell. He lunged half-cocked into the nearest side street.

"Wait, I remember," I said. "Somebody said you were tending bar or something like that. Was it in Shinjuku?"

"Yup. Let's start here." He stopped with his hand on a door, under a sign that said PALOMA, and turned to me and shouted "KA-BOOM!" as he opened it. I followed him into the dim interior. A woman's voice greeted us.

"Oh my. 'Ka-boom' again?"

Komai seemed to be a regular here. Maybe "ka-boom" was how he announced that he was drunk. "Good evening!" the woman added in a more formal tone when she noticed me.

"He's a friend. I ran into him outside." Komai floated onto one of the bar stools and planted an elbow on the counter.

"Don't you want a table?" the woman said.

"Nah, this is good."

I took the next stool as the two of them talked. The round-faced bartender looked about thirty. He smiled warmly and said, "Are you having what the sensei is having?"

Komai asked me what I wanted. I said I'd have what he was having and took another close look at this face I hadn't seen in twenty-plus years. "You're a 'sensei'?"

He started belting out "Sensei," which was just then at the top of the charts. "Sensei, sensei, I'm a sensei too . . ."

"Always clowning around. Here's your washcloth." A girl in a light summer kimono passed us hot towels from behind.

"What kind of sensei are you?" I asked.

The girl behind me almost squealed. "Are you *really* friends? Sensei, is he really your friend?"

"Sure. How long has it been?" Komai said as he wiped his face.

"Since we graduated. About twenty-two years."

"Wow. Twenty-two already," he said with feeling. Our

drinks arrived. He lifted his. "Well..." We touched glasses.

It was brandy and water. I hadn't asked for it, but it was something I'd been drinking a lot at the time. Somehow it seemed auspicious.

"Then I guess you wouldn't know," the girl said to me. She put a hand on our shoulders, almost standing between us. "Oh, you've got to tell me. What kind of student was Komai-san?"

"You went to Waseda, right?" he said.

"Yeah."

"What do you do now?"

"Peddle stocks."

"Been doing it for a while?"

"Yeah, since I got out of school."

He said "Hmm," apparently impressed, and took a sip of his brandy.

"Sensei?" The bartender grinned.

"Yeah?"

"You had a run-in with Senda, didn't you?"

"Word travels fast."

"It doesn't have far to travel." The bartender laughed.

"It was my fault. All my fault," Komai murmured. He brightened suddenly and almost shouted, "How's the old gang? You see them at reunions, don't you?" His eyes were shining. He looked like a student again.

"I went two years ago. It was crowded. Remember Ono?"

"Ono the super student, yeah."

"He organized the last reunion. He might be handling the next one too. You should at least give him your address." Komai had never shown his face at one of these gatherings.

"What's he doing now?"

"He works at City Hall."

Komai said "Hmm" again and took another sip.

"I guess you must've been really into literature when you were a student," the girl said to him. She seemed intensely interested.

"Komai? Into literature?" I laughed. I'd known him since middle school, but he'd never been much for critical argument. He was addicted to old-time comedy and movies, but his critiques of what he liked were so shallow, he could've just said "terrific" and saved himself the time. When others ventured an opinion that struck him as unsophisticated, he'd make stupid jokes instead of engaging with them. He was about as far from my picture of a literature buff as I could've imagined.

"He used to throw the bull around," I added. "I don't know about now, but back then he used to love putting people on. Maybe he's doing that to you?"

"No, that's impossible." The girl was dead earnest. From the look on her face, I was well on my way to her shit list.

"Look, it's okay." Komai tried to calm her down. "He's right, I used to bullshit a lot."

The girl didn't seem convinced. "All right," she said finally. "I'll show you." She walked into the kitchen.

Komai shrugged apologetically. "I got into a fist fight for the first time in a while."

He must've been through a lot in twenty-two years, but the care and hardship seemed to melt away. I was looking at the same half-delinquent I'd known as a teenager. He'd always been young. It was a mystery how he could go on year after year looking, acting, and talking like a child.

"Still young as ever," I said.

"Yup. I was in the bar business a long time, you know."

My thoughts went back to those days. Nearly all of us had been bound for college, but Komai took himself off that track early on. Our third-year classes had been focused like a laser on the entrance exams. I used to look out the window and see him walking around the schoolyard, chasing a soccer ball or hitting a tennis ball against a wall, all by himself.

I used to envy him for having it so easy. The school was going to graduate him anyway. Since he wouldn't be sitting the exams, he had no use for the classes we were taking.

"Look!" the girl said proudly in my ear. She spread two magazines out on the counter. "Komai-san is writing a novel."

I looked at the magazines and almost choked. The whole thing was nutty. "This is you?" I said. There it was—KOMAI KEISUKE in inch-high print.

"It's no big deal." He was embarrassed. That was better proof than anything that he really was a writer.

"Take that away, you idiot," he said petulantly. The girl saw the look on his face and took the magazines away.

"What are you so upset about?"

"Novelists write lies, you know? I've been a liar from way back." He was talking the way he had in high school. Maybe that was how he amused himself.

"What made you want to write a novel?"

"Why not? You sell stocks, don't you?"

"I majored in business. What else would I do with myself?"

Komai shrugged. "What do you major in to be a bartender?"

The man behind the counter smiled. "I majored in administration."

"See? This fool went to university to become a bartender. He's a lot weirder than me."

"Everyone's different," I said. "But how did you get started writing?"

"I copied somebody."

"Who?"

"A customer. I was a bartender for a long time, right? You meet all kinds that way."

"I've got to let Ono know. No one would guess you'd be writing novels."

"Pretty cool, huh?"

"Sure."

"And you made it to selling stocks."

"That's a strange way to put it." I laughed awkwardly.

"I mean, having a novelist in the group is better than having a criminal."

"Okay, I guess." I wasn't sure what he was getting at.

"Something wrong with writing novels instead of going to university?" Komai said jokingly.

"No, but it seems a bit hard to believe."

"Yeah, you're right. It's no good." Now he sounded depressed.

"I was kidding. Don't take it seriously."

"No . . ." He stared at the counter and shook his head. "That's not what I mean. Nothing you say bothers me. It's not that. I'm a jerk. I shouldn't be writing novels."

He downed the rest of his drink and slid the glass toward the bartender for a refill.

"Are you all right?" I asked.

"I'm sorry. After all these years . . ."

"No problem. But what's gotten into you?" Now he had me worried about him.

"Everyone's pissed off at me."

"Who's 'everyone'?"

"Andromeda's Mama. Ue-chan at Zelkova. Senda at The Pot Still . . ."

I didn't recognize any of those names. But whatever was wrong, it was enough to bring Komai to tears.

"You asked me why I started writing novels..."

He still seemed depressed. Half hoping to cheer him up, I'd been knocking them back pretty steadily and getting drunk. We'd moved to a table in the back. I'd stopped worrying about the last train. After trading stories with him about the old days, I got sucked into hearing the story of his life.

"Yeah, I did ask you."

"I get that a lot. 'Why did you write a novel?' It's hard to answer. If someone asked you why you started selling stocks, you probably couldn't say much, other than it was an accident."

"You're right about that."

"Same with me. There was nothing else to do. I was cornered. But the truth doesn't sound good, you know? If I told people I wrote a novel—poof! just like that—it might sound pretty stuck up."

"Maybe. I've never been interested in fiction. I'm not sure how people would react."

"Right, me neither. I never know how people will react. But to really explain why I started writing, I'd have to go back a long way. The truth is, I remember you guys."

"The gang from high school?"

"Yeah. You and Isomura and Inoue and Aizaki and Yokota. Everybody."

"No kidding." This was a surprise.

"I didn't go to that school to get into some university. But everybody else did. I guess I picked up their attitude. Then one day it hit me. I couldn't go. My family didn't have money. When I saw I'd never go to university, exam prep had already started. You probably don't know this, but they let me skip classes."

"Sure, I knew about that."

"I could've taken them. I wasn't shut out. But I never

felt like going. I knew they'd let me graduate. No one in my shoes would've wanted to go to class."

"I remember. You were always in the schoolyard."

"All the time. Yeah, I was always there, with no one else around. I wanted to piss people off a little. But it was lonely."

"The rest of us envied you."

He laughed. "Back then there was a boxing gym near the school. Guys from the mob used to hang out there. A serious student like you probably didn't even know it was there."

I tried to remember the place, but he was right. I couldn't remember ever seeing it.

"I started training there."

"Really? You were boxing?" This was news to me.

"That's right. Maybe I felt alienated. Spending time around guys from the mob was oddly refreshing. I got in the ring. Put on the trunks, the gloves . . . I wanted to be a competitor. I wanted to make lots of money while the rest of you guys were in school spending it. But I found out that being a boxer takes luck and determination. Taking punches hurt, too. I got knocked out over and over until I was fed up. Punches to the face are one thing, but body blows are the worst. I got sick of it."

The last time I'd seen Komai was after graduation, but by that time we were living in different universes. I saw him every day at school, but he'd already disappeared. None of us had any idea he was boxing.

During his time at the gym, Komai made friends with the mobsters hanging out there. Then one of them offered him a part-time job tending bar in place that served the occupation forces. The Korean War was getting under way, and there were a lot of bars in Ginza catering to GIs. They'd have to go back to the front line when their leave was up, so they spent money like there was no tomorrow.

Komai didn't know a thing about bartending, but it sounded like he picked it up quickly. He got two hundred yen a day working afternoons at a little counter bar in Ginza's Second District.

The girls who worked at those bars were very different from hostesses now. They were working to eat, not to have a nice lifestyle. They were down-to-earth and playful. Each one had her sad history but was ready anytime for banter and silly jokes and laughter. Still, when something triggered a bout of temper or weeping, they would pour out the whole long story of how they ended up hostessing for GIs.

Komai witnessed all of this and became fascinated with the women and their stories. The hostess whose GI lover was killed, and who become someone's mistress out of despair. The carefree hostess who captured the heart of a black soldier and crossed the ocean without a backward look. The brassy bar girl who tricked an officer into buying her her own place. As he worked with this cast of characters, Komai lost interest in any other world. He became a citizen of the night.

"You guys are fools 'cause you're smart."

Komai interrupted his story about tending bar for GIs with this enigmatic remark

"I don't think of myself as smart," I said. "But what's that supposed to mean, anyway?"

"You think you can reason everything out. But everyone's a fool. We're all fools. You don't know the world is full of fools, so you try to do the smart thing. Look at everyone here. That bartender, the girls, they're all fools. Fools are good people, you know. They might talk about how they should've done things differently, but they have no regrets. Not really."

"I wonder."

"It's true. Deep down they know they're fools. If they

do something foolish, they know that was the only thing they could've done. So they never really regret their mistakes. They go through life blowing one opportunity after another, and the results pile up, and they come to a place like this. How long have you been selling stocks?"

"This is my eighteenth year."

"I'm surprised you made it that long without failing out of it. It's great you stayed on track. I've been off track since I left the gym. Smart people regret it when they screw up, but if you end up like me, you drop the whole regret thing. When you're a fool, screwups come with the territory. After Ginza, I didn't just tend bar. I even got sidetracked from bartending, drifted from one place to another. Ending up in Shinjuku was part of that. I made it hard for myself to stay in Ginza, so I caught a streetcar and got out into the country . . .

"Well, I didn't go all that far. Shinjuku used to be a pretty low-class place compared to Ginza. Now it's rising, and Ginza is going downhill, so things are about right. But in the early fifties, this whole area was pretty seedy. My first gig was at an old bar pretty close to here. They didn't know what a cocktail was."

"Aren't cocktails the same wherever you go?"

"The ones that've been around forever, the classic cocktails, they're the same. Mixing alcohol is the same anywhere. But people in Shinjuku'd never heard of them. Everybody drank straight.

"So somebody'd mix up something and name it after a hit movie. The customers didn't know you could only get certain drinks in certain bars. They'd go to another bar and order them. If you didn't know what they were talking about, they'd throw insults at you. Imagine somebody asking you to mix up a 'Tomorrow is Too Late.' It was pathetic."

"Was that really a drink?"

"Sure was. There were all kinds. I thought up one myself."

"What was it?"

"'Heartless City.' Just water in a cocktail glass. 'That'll be a thousand yen,' I used to joke."

"Pretty stupid."

"You think? It *was* stupid. But as I got used to Shinjuku, I got to really like living here. That bar was where I met my first author."

"A novelist? Which one?"

"Not a novelist exactly. He taught high school literature. Name was Iida. He edited a little literary journal. When I met him, he was working hard on his first book."

"Not a real novelist? Okay."

"Come on, I thought it was a big deal. He already had a solid job, but he was aiming for something higher. I got to like him quite a bit. He didn't have much money though. There was this hostess at the bar named Yasuko. Delicate, kind of lonely-looking. But she was a good woman. She was married to Iida-san."

"A high school teacher with a bar hostess wife? That's pretty offbeat."

"There must've been a reason. She was pretty, too. Anyway, Iida used to bring his friends to the bar all the time. Now that I think of it, they must've been connected to his journal. He was the leader, he used to get everyone together for drinks. Yasuko wasn't that outgoing, but when her husband and his friends came in, she took good care of them, like she was the Mama. She wanted Iida-san to make it as a novelist."

"And that's how you got the idea of writing novels yourself?"

Komai shook his head. "I was rooting for him, that's all. I never read anything he wrote. But seeing him and

Yasuko working so hard together somehow made me envy them. It got to me, in a way. When he'd drink at the bar, I'd 'forget' to charge him for some of the drinks, or make it easier for Yasuko to spend time with him and his friends. That was about all I could do to help. But I wanted at least one of us fools to succeed." He scratched his head diffidently and laughed.

"Iida-san knew what he was doing. He wasn't like I am, not at all. There aren't too many people like that. Yasuko too—she was straight-arrow, a good woman. I didn't think Iida could've done any better."

"Good night." Three of the hostesses left the bar together.

"Is it that late already?" I looked at my watch.

"Forget about the last train. We've still got lots to talk about." A few of the hostesses were still hanging on. There was no sign the bar was closing.

"This Iida—he was successful, then?" I was still very curious about how Komai had started writing. I couldn't quite make the connection between Keisuke the bartender and Keisuke the novelist.

"As far as I know. One day Yasuko came in really excited and told us he'd quit his teaching job. She said he'd won some kind of prize they give to new writers. He was on his way. It wasn't just me, everyone was rooting for them. We all liked them, you know? And to be honest, the Mama and the bartenders thought it would be a mistake for a woman like Yasuko to spend too much time in this town."

"Why?"

"She'd become a fool. One day she'd do something foolish and become a fool. Anyone who gets to know this world figures that out, sooner or later. For some reason Shinjuku wasn't good for her. She might get a bit of a break, but never anything big. It was a dead end. A place where people with nowhere else to go hang out. It would've just held her back."

"Are you sure? You went into the business after high school. But you ended up getting out of it, didn't you?"

"I got out, sure. But they say when you kick an addiction, it hurts like hell. I didn't get out because of luck or anything I did. I got kicked out."

Komai finally quit and moved to another bar. Shinjuku was growing fast in the fifties. More and more bars were opening up, and they started doing things the way they were done in Ginza. Because he knew how the bar business worked in both parts of town, he was in demand. After stints at several bars, he fell in love and got married.

"To tell the truth, she was a lot taller than me." Komai moved a flat palm above his head from side to side, laughing. "Stiletto heels were popular then. Dressed for work she looked even taller."

"She was a hostess?"

"What do you think?"

"You worked together, then."

"It wasn't fun. I never thought I'd be doing it. Bartenders and hostesses get together, they're still bartenders and hostesses. You register at city hall. Her last name changes. Okay, now she's your wife.

"But that's not how it felt. We were living together, that's all. It would sound romantic if I said we made it official. Or maybe it would sound stupid. Some people'd think it was. 'Did you really have to go get married?' and so forth. Stick around here till closing. You'll see bartenders going home with hostesses. And the guy you think is a bartender just might be the owner."

I couldn't help turning to study the bartenders. Komai laughed. "You look like you're in a haunted house."

"You can't be too careful, can you?"

"Not if you want to stay on top of things. All the average person wants to do is come in, have a drink, and get buzzed."

"And you're still with her?"

"Don't be stupid. Not even tombstones last forever."

"Come on, get to the point. So you broke up, then."

"Husbands and wives... When things are good, it's like you're sitting next to each other on a train, going toward the same destination. The next thing you know, you're looking out the window at a train on the next track over. You can see her sitting there looking back at you. If the tracks diverge, she's out of sight instantly. No time for goodbyes. You're smart, so you probably don't have a clue about that."

"I've been on the same train with my wife for fourteen years now."

"Kids?"

"The oldest is twelve."

"How many?"

"Three."

"It's a terrible thing, isn't it?"

"Yeah." As soon as I realized what I'd said—Komai's comment struck me as spot on—I laughed awkwardly. "But what happened to Iida and Yasuko?"

He stared into the distance.

"They separated. It was bad. It was really bad. They were both smart, on the surface anyway. I guess a pair of fools would've handled it better. Iida got his new writer prize. He thought he was on his way. But it didn't happen. He'd quit his job at the school. He wrote and wrote, but it didn't pay the bills, and Yasuko was always a bit neurotic, so it must've been more than he could stand. He ended up telling fortunes outside Hanazono Shrine."

"There's always someone standing there reading palms."

"Yeah, that's what he did. No start-up capital needed."

"He made a mistake, quitting his job."

"See? Regrets. If he'd never made a mistake, he wouldn't've ended up in Night City. Way before he quit his job and became a palm reader, he and Yasuko took a wrong turn somewhere. Maybe things were off course even before they got married." He stared down at the table.

"I guess I can understand how Yasuko felt, but still, it was a typical case. I don't want to blame her, but women are a bit like clever mice in a way. They're weak, so when things go bad, they look out for themselves. When their ship—the guy—starts going down, they run for safety.

"Mice can't talk, but women—they've got lots of excuses for leaving. 'It's your fault,' 'I put up with you for so long,' 'Do something!' They're blowing smoke. When things start going sideways, men get clingy or blame the woman or sulk. Maybe the woman doesn't get that he's sending up a distress rocket, or maybe she just pretends not to. Either way, she'll jump ship to save herself. When a woman leaves you, it's usually not just about you and her. There's a bigger problem. That's why she cuts and runs."

Komai studied me closely and grinned.

"It's like bankers and stock peddlers. They're only interested in you when you're flush."

"Come on, don't say that."

"Yasuko was like that job you have. When she figured her husband was going to fail, she sold her stock in him."

"You're gonna piss me off—"

"I'm talking about Yasuko."

I laughed uncomfortably.

"You know what happens when a woman sells her stock?"

"She buys a different stock?"

"See? You do know how this works."

"Goddamn it!"

"Exactly. She cheated on him. She left and came back, over and over, and every time they had a knock-down drag-out. You know how the story ends. Iida's alone. Ex-school teacher, aspiring novelist, up-and-comer going nowhere. So he ends up reading palms in the shadows at Hanazono Shrine. The sad thing is, he tried to make a go of it. He decided he'd be the best roadside fortune teller around. Isn't that sad? I mean, everyone in Shinjuku's a fool, but that doesn't mean somebody like Iida-san had to be one too. At first we avoided the shrine 'cause we hated to see him standing there. But he worked so hard at it that afterward, I went and had him read my palm."

"Did his reading come true?"

"He told me I'd break up with my woman. *That* was ridiculous. He didn't know his woman would leave *him*, but with me he got it exactly right. There's this old story—maybe you know it?" Komai looked strangely sober.

"This fortune teller dies suddenly. He comes back as a ghost and tells people, 'You're going to die too . . . You're going to die too . . .' Know what? He was always right."

"What happened to the hostess? Yasuko?"

"Vanished. Whereabouts unknown. Some guy took her in. About now, she's probably a good wife someplace. That's what happens to women who get out of the business. In your world, vanishing without a trace isn't a good sign, but it is for us. If you never hear from someone again, it means she's doing all right. And that's fine. Nobody thinks about her unless she's living someplace nearby."

"I see. What about you? You broke up with your wife, I guess?"

"Yeah. It was pretty rough. We were living next to the

Imperial Gardens. She didn't come home. At first I hated it. I'd hear footsteps coming down the street, I couldn't sleep. I couldn't help being angry. It was pitiful. If things get miserable enough and stupid enough, you want to die.

"But there's always the bottle. Revenge drinking. I'd get drunk by myself. The drunker I got, the lonelier I felt. One night I was so lonely I got chased by some dogs and thought I was gonna get killed."

"Huh?"

"I went over the wall. Snuck into the Imperial Gardens. There was a full moon out. It's a big place, no one around. Anyway I was drunk, so I ran around that huge lawn yelling my head off. 'Fuck you, asshole,' that kind of thing. Then a pack of dogs comes at me. They weren't all strays either. Some of them they keep chained in the daytime and let them run around after dark. They chased me, barking and yapping. A big pack of dogs."

"A pack of dogs . . ." I couldn't help laughing. It was hard to picture Komai the novelist, but Komai dumped by his wife and chased by dogs—that I could imagine. I told him what I was thinking. He laughed happily.

"I know, I know. I'm perfect for it. I ran like hell and hoisted myself up on the wall. When I looked down, the dogs were looking up at me, wagging their tails. Shinjuku dogs for sure, I thought. They were just having me on."

"Didn't you know? The wagging tail is the giveaway."

"I never lived in a house with a yard, so I haven't spent much time around dogs."

"You've had a lot of strange experiences."

"Next time you lose at love, get something to chase you so you can run like hell, so you gasp for breath and fear for your life. That'll teach you that losing at love is no big deal."

"I'm forty."

"Then you've got plenty of time. Try it. It's fun."

"So what about your novel? I've been drinking all night waiting to hear the story."

"I wrote a novel."

"When?"

"Right after my run in the park. I didn't know the guy she ran off with—maybe he was a poet or a painter or something. Anyway, he was talented and popular. Not the type a bartender could go up against. I didn't want to anyway. I was like a punctured balloon. I got to hate my job too. I was a fool, my buddies were fools, all the fools got together and built Fooltown. I used to be happy, thinking it was my town.

"But the ones who really have fun, those are the smart people. They drop by Fooltown anytime, not meaning any harm, of course. They get a taste of it and leave. Back home with their buddies they have a good laugh about how much fun the fools are. That's the hardest thing about being a fool, when you finally get that. I was deflated, all out of air. Weightless. I was like that for a while, deflated and limp, but that's the good thing about being a fool. You can't do one thing for too long. I got tired of being tired. I started wanting to do something over-the-top foolish."

Komai took a drink and put the glass down quickly. "So I wrote it. I wrote the novel. They say ignorance knows no fear, but it wasn't quite like that. It was more like a blockhead who trips over his feet and wants to do it again, just for laughs."

He seemed to remember something then; his face fell. "Yeah, that's how it was. I wanted to sprawl flat on my face, just for laughs. But that novel got me run out of my beloved Fooltown. Shouldna done it."

"But you're making a living from it, right?"

He didn't answer immediately. As I watched, a vein stood out on his forehead.

"A living. That's rich. Everyone here is a fool, but they're making a living. I made a living tending bar, not that I bragged about it. I didn't have to write a novel to make a living."

"I get that, but being a writer is better than tending bar, isn't it?"

"Sure. Most of all, it looks good." His tone turned harsh. "Of course it looks good. But working in a place like this is better. You know, you worry too much about status. Is looking good really so much better? What happens if you don't look good? Does it matter?"

"Doesn't it? Sorry, but I don't see how you can think it doesn't. I'd love to know why."

"I don't know myself. But I have a feeling it doesn't matter. I think I screwed up somewhere again. It's a hunch, not logic. Somehow I've ended up in a very strange place. If I don't get back to where I used to be pretty soon, something bad's sure to happen. That's how I feel."

"Good evening . . ."

A man came through the door. Komai saw him, and his expression changed. He looked unhappy, like he'd just been cornered by a bill collector.

"I heard the sensei's here," the man said to the bartender. He was clearly in the same business; he was wearing a bow tie. He looked about the same age as Komai and me. A narrow strip of adhesive tape ran along the edge of his jaw.

"Sensei's right here," Komai called.

"There you are, Koma-san. Still going at it in a place like this?" The man approached our table with a gentle smile, as though he were humoring a child. Komai introduced him a bit reluctantly.

"This is Senda. He works at a bar called The Pot Still. It's nearby. He's a character in a lot of my stories."

"Nice to meet you," Senda said. "You should try our

place. It's lots more interesting than this." The guys behind the bar laughed. They seemed to know him well.

"Is The Pot Still that interesting?" I asked.

"Yes. We have dolls that pee when you squeeze their breasts."

"Sounds like a strange bar."

"I found them at an adult toy store. Sometimes they sell things that are quite educational."

"You call that educational?"

"We have more than dolls. They've all gone home now, but we have real women too. They don't pee when you squeeze them, though."

"Hey." Komai sounded sullen. "What d'you want? You want something, right?"

"I heard you were here, so I thought I'd let you buy me a drink. After all, you're the sensei." Senda went to the counter and the barman poured him a whisky.

"He and I worked together a long time," Komai explained. Senda came back to our table, whisky on the rocks in hand.

"Koma-san, Ue-chan, and me," he said to me. "The three of us made Shinjuku what it is."

"Get off it."

"After I finish this, let's go somewhere else."

Komai's face lit up. "Shall we?"

"Let's."

I was starting to get curious about what was going on between these two men.

"Oh, by the way. We got in a fistfight tonight," Komai said.

"You mentioned it. This is who you were fighting with?"

"Yeah. It was over Iida-san."

I glanced at Senda's jaw.

"It was your fault, Koma-san," Senda said. He touched

his jaw and smiled. "I found out that Iida-san was killed by a car a few days ago. He was drunk. It was his fault."

"I heard about it at Sen-chan's bar," Komai said. "I was drunk. I guess I kinda blew it off."

"You shouted your usual 'ka-boom' when you came in, so I knew you were drunk."

"Okay, I made a bad joke. I said he must've known he'd get killed since he was such a great fortune teller."

"Yes, you were drunk."

"Yep. Still, my bad. Me and Sen-chan used to stand behind the bar listening to Iida go on and on about literature. We really wanted him to make it. Be a real novelist. Then he had all those troubles, and ended up on the street reading palms. I guess my writing novels was kind of a rebound off that."

Komai glanced quickly at Senda. "He thought I'd start bawling when I heard the news. So he's really nervous when he tells me. But I don't bat an eye. Man, he flew off the handle. Calls me inhuman, a narcissist, tells me to get the hell out and never come back. It was rough."

"What did you expect?" Senda said. "I mean, after all . . ."

I was starting to understand how these men saw things. Senda wasn't upset at Komai's cool response. What had infuriated him was Komai's joke, and the lack of love it showed for a fellow fool—a fool Komai had been going on about all night to me.

"I know how you feel." I spoke straight from my gut. The most important thing was to cherish one's blunders in life and understand and sympathize with the blunders of others.

This was what Komai had been telling me all evening. He was right; I'd tried to live the "smart" way. I was scornful of screwups and hated to cut people slack, that had been a basic principle of mine. But now I saw my whole life for what it was—a chain of accidents and mistimed decisions.

"Sen-chan was giving it to me so bad I lost my temper. Knowing it was my fault made it even worse. I said let's go outside goddamn it, and we started fighting in the street like two kids."

"That was no fistfight. *You* punched *me*, that's all." Senda touched his jaw again.

"Everybody came running. Ue-chan pinned me from behind. When they asked what we were fighting about, Sen-chan told them the whole story."

"Why not? You hit me. I was upset," Senda said a bit peevishly.

"When they heard what happened, everybody was knocked back. They gave me hell." Komai's voice was tired and sad. "They were right. I was acting stupid. I got caught up with writing and spending time with other people and forgot the most important thing of all. I'm just a jerk."

"Shall we?" Senda said to me. I stood up. The two men's view of life seemed to match my alcoholic buzz perfectly. I vaguely sensed that by morning, my understanding of their world might be gone along with the buzz. But just then I very much wanted to be part of it.

By the time we got to the next bar, Senda and Komai were making plans to visit Iida's grave. Afterward, Komai dropped me off at home. When I saw the scowl on my wife's face as I opened the door, I was ready to forgive both of us for our screwups. I was that far gone.

As for Komai, I haven't seen him since.

Contributors

Hanmura Ryō (半村 良, pseudonym of Kiyono Heitarō, 1933–2002), born in Tokyo's Katsushika Ward, spent thirty years moving from job to job, including manning reception desks at love hotels and bartending in cabarets. He debuted as an author in 1962, but was little heard-from until 1971, when his Seiun Award-winning novel *Ishi no Ketsumyaku (Veins of Stone)* reintroduced him as a pioneer in the *denki shōsetsu* subgenre of dark, often historically based fantasy. In 1975, he became the first SF author to win the Naoki Prize, with the non-SF novel you hold in your hands. Throughout the 1970s, he produced new works at a furious pace, and continued writing SF, fantasy, and historical novels until 2001, earning the Nihon SF Taishō Award in 1988 and the Shibata Renzaburō Prize in 1993.

Jim Hubbert is a translator of Japanese based in Tokyo. His translations include works by Miyabe Miyuki, Ueda Sayuri, Project Itoh, and Ogawa Issui.

Torontonian **Johnny Wales** has lived off and on (mostly on) in Japan since his first trip there in 1975. Johnny is an illustrator, sculptor, animator and, well, lets just say he is always making things.

He and his wife Chieko and their pooch Kyla live in an old farmhouse on Sado Island in the Sea of Japan.

johnny-wales.com

Lightning Source UK Ltd.
Milton Keynes UK
UKHW010750090120
356646UK00001B/28/P